QUEEN OF Always

SHERRY FICKLIN

CLEAN TEEN PUBLISHING

QUEEN OF *Always*

ISBN: 978-1-63422-141-2
Cover Design by: Marya Heiman
Typography by: Courtney Nuckels
Editing by: Cynthia Shepp

FOR LINDA BETH FRISTOE.
THANK YOU DOESN'T SEEM LIKE ENOUGH.

For more information about our content disclosure, please utilize the QR code above with your smartphone or visit us at

www.cleanteenpublishing.com.

"To tempt and to be tempted are things very nearly allied - whenever feeling has anything to do in the matter, no sooner is it excited than we have already gone vastly farther than we are aware of."
~Catherine the Great

Author's note

In keeping with the real life of Catherine the Great, this story is filled with both violence and sensuality. It's not intended for young or sensitive readers. Though I took many liberties with the narrative, I have tried, always, to remain true to the compelling, strong woman who was Catherine the Great. Though it is not completely historically accurate, I hope you will enjoy this final piece in her saga, as remained by a great fan.

Chapter

ONE

My eyelids are heavy when a rough shake pulls me from the depth of my slumber. I blink against the dim candlelight and young Dashka, my newest lady-in-waiting, stands over me, her expression near panic. I sit up quickly.

"What is it, Dash?"

A slip girl, Dashka is the youngest of the Vorontsova sisters. She looks so much like my dear friend Rina, with her blonde locks and sharply sloped nose—even the shape of her eyes betray their relation—that it had been impossible not to immediately love her. She'd come to Oranienbaum Palace when Rina first fell ill some months ago, and she has been serving me in her sister's stead since.

"It's Ekaterina, Your Grace, she's asking for you," she says, her voice as fragile as a silk thread. I pat her arm gently, and she helps me from bed. A cold chill washes over me. It's as I feared. My dearest friend has been ill for some time. Each day, I watch as she grows smaller, paler, and weaker. I've been praying for a miracle, all the while knowing that I don't deserve one.

Not after what I've done.

Dressed and quickly groomed, I emerge from my chamber into the eerie stillness of the hall. The palace is unusually quiet at this hour. There have been no feasts roaring into the night, not since Peter's last tantrum, in which he publically wished his aunt, the Empress Elizabeth, would "*Die already and be done with it.*"

Of course, word of his careless speech reached the ears of his incapacitated but still very alert aunt, who quickly withdrew court funds for such events, plunging Oranienbaum Palace, or the *little court* as they have taken to calling it, into a state of eternal dreariness.

I can't say I'm sorry, though. Whenever I feel in need of entertainment or distraction, I simply host games, songs, and dancing in my private rooms, which allows me the freedom to pick and choose those who attend, granting me a reprieve from Peter and his garish mistress Elizavetta. Or at least, I had done so, until Rina took ill. Since that day, a dark cloud has settled over my heart and there is no escape from it.

As I walk down the hall toward the room where Rina is resting, I spare a moment to glance behind me, putting a face to the third set of feet hitting the ground behind me. I'm not surprised to see my personal guard there. My ever-present shadow and devoted protector, Grigori barely leaves my side these days. Despite the hour, his dark blue uniform is pressed, his hair combed back and tied at his neck with a leather lace, and his sword is on his hip.

"Don't you ever sleep, Grigori?" I ask lightly. In Sergei's absence, all pretense of formality between us has fallen away, and Grigori has become more a friend than simply a guard. I often invite him to my private gathering where he pretends, quite gracefully, to lose to me at cards.

"Not on nights like tonight," he says cryptically, his brow furrowed over his blue eyes. "There's a wrongness tonight. I can feel it in my bones. Dark skies on the horizon."

I just shake my head. It seems recently that my life is nothing but a series of dark skies. It's been over a year since I poisoned the empress' tea, and she still manages to cling to life. Over a year since my lover Sergei was sent away, leaving me without respite from the tedium of my existence. Over a year since my child was ripped from my arms.

Dark skies aren't on the horizon at all. They are firmly settled directly overhead.

Pausing outside the door, I take a deep breath, preparing myself for the worst.

Struck down in her youth with the wasting sickness, Rina has been clinging to life by the frailest thread. Her fever has raged out of control for weeks as she refuses to eat, literally fading before my eyes. And now, now the coughing has begun, always sprinkled with spittle and blood. The physician says there is no more he can do, that it is in God's hands. Now Archbishop Novgorod waits in eerie stillness outside her door, no doubt having just administered her last rites. He bows when I approach, his wizened face dark beneath his long, gray beard. I acknowledge him but say nothing. He alone has taken my confession and knows my greatest sin. My greatest weakness, my utmost sorrow. He has been an immense comfort, if only in his firm belief that I am deserving of redemption. He urges me to pray for it, but I haven't the heart.

Or perhaps, I am too proud for regret. Either way, I am glad he is here.

When I open the door, the desire to rush to Rina and take her hand is powerful. But I know I cannot. There is a chair, not far from her bedside, under the window, which lets white moonlight stream in, and I know I must take my seat there. I am the Grand Duchess of Russia, and I cannot risk my health for even a moment. To do so would mean leaving my son Paul, and my country, unprotected and in the hands of my idiot husband Peter and his cruel aunt, the Empress Elizabeth. For that alone, I remain distant, though everything inside of me is demanding to hold her.

Glancing around the room, I see Alexander

standing in the back alcove with his arms folded around the little boy clinging to his chest. The boy is bigger than I remember, his face still chubby in his youth, his hair the same dark, wavy mass as his father. He looks tired and perhaps a bit confused. Seeing me, he smiles hesitantly.

Many afternoons have been whiled away playing with him in the nursery at Oranienbaum, chasing each other through the massive gardens on the estate grounds, or even just singing sweet lullabies with him and his fair-haired mother. He has been, in so many ways, a surrogate for my own son. Now he looks at me hopefully, and I cannot help but offer him a reassuring smile. He's my godson, after all, and I cannot bear to allow even this to darken his sweet spirit.

Alexander, however, stands stoic. His dark hair is disheveled, his eyes deep and dark with exhaustion. He's pale, paler than I've ever seen his normally olive-toned skin, and his mouth is set in a hard line. He glances at me only briefly before returning his eyes to her. My own gaze follows his.

I can barely tell her pallid skin from the linens. Her color is gone, even her normally golden hair is faded to a pale, shimmering white. Her eyes are open, only just, and she lets her head roll to the side, smiling at me through dry, cracked lips.

"Your Grace," she begins. "Catherine. I'm so glad to see you."

"And I'm glad to see you as well. But you should be resting," I urge.

She licks her lips. Her voice is faint and wispy, like a summer breeze. "Alexander, may I have a moment with my friend?"

He shifts the boy in his arms, nodding once before turning sharply and leaving.

"What is it, Rina?" I ask. "What can I do?" The question is vague, but it's all I can manage because I know there is nothing. The knowledge pains me more than I thought possible.

She smiles again. "The doctor says I don't have long now." I open my mouth to say that is nonsense, but she continues. "He's right. I can feel it. It's a heaviness. Feels a bit like falling asleep, actually. The pain is mostly gone now."

As if to betray her words, she begins to cough violently, covering her mouth with a bloodstained rag. I stand, but she waves me back down.

"It grieves me to think of the world without you in it," I say honestly, struggling to hold my voice firm. "I need you."

"You will be fine. You are so strong, Sophie. So much stronger than you think."

I flinch at my given name, spoken for the first time in so long. Everyone has taken to calling me Catherine now, even Sergei. It's difficult to hear, to be reminded of that simpler time.

"Tell me, how is Sergei?" she asks, changing the

subject.

I exhale sharply. "I honestly don't know. He's been traveling, at the empress' behest. He was back at Winter Palace only days before she sent him away again. She thinks to keep him far from me, I think, and far from Paul." I don't have to explain why. Rina alone knows the truth of Paul's paternity. She knows it is likely Sergei, and not Peter, who fathered the child. I only wish I could see my son again, to look into his small face and be sure. Surely, he will look like Sergei, and then there will be no doubt. Even as I think it, my heart sinks. "Truthfully, I haven't had word from him in weeks. His letters grow infrequent and impersonal. I fear he may be tired of me, or worse, he may have found another."

"I doubt that very much," she says, her eyes drooping a little more. "It seems to me that your love is like a fine brandy to men. Once they've had a taste of it, they will crave it all their days."

I frown, instantly feeling the sting of her accusation. Alexander, her husband, had nearly been my lover. We had, in the foolishness of youth, nearly run away together, so madly infatuated were we. It was the empress' rage that forced him and Rina to marry, all to punish me for even considering abandoning my obligation to her—to Russia.

"Oh, I didn't mean to upset you," she adds softly. "It's true though. You shouldn't worry so."

I rub my eye with my finger. "I'm sorry," is all I

can think to say. It doesn't feel like enough.

"Don't be sorry. I loved you too. Sometimes, I think I even loved you best, better than all the others, because I loved you enough to share you." She grins. "Silly, jealous boys."

"I never wanted you to be unhappy," I say, standing and facing the window.

She coughs again. "Why on earth would you think I am unhappy? I have a wonderful husband and a beautiful son, and my dearest friend is here with me, at the end of the night."

I turn back to her. "I can't help but think you deserved so much better than this."

She shakes her head just a bit. "I have no complaints and no regrets. You should know that. Life isn't just beginnings and endings. It's the things in the middle that matter most. And my middle has been wonderful."

I fight back the tears pooling behind my eyes.

"Make sure he knows that I loved him, that I loved you both. Make sure he knows it was enough," she says, her voice rattling deep in her chest.

"I will," I promise, facing her again.

Her eyes flutter closed for the last time, and I hear the hiss as her final breath escapes her body. It cuts through me like a knife, leaving nothing but a hollow ache in its wake.

I cover my face with my hand, doubling over against the pain and slipping from the chair onto the floor. Sitting like that until I can gain my feet again, I stare at her, so small in the large bed.

I didn't deserve her. Rina was so much more than a lady-in-waiting; she was my closest friend. She deserved a manor in the country, a husband who thought the sun rose and set on her face, and an army of children nipping at her heels. She deserved all that and so much more.

Bolting from the room, I run into the hall, right into Elizavetta. Her red hair hangs in limp, lifeless waves around her pudgy face. Her eyes are round, like her sister's, only in a murky shade of green and rimmed in red. Her pale pink satin gown is wrinkled and disheveled. I can only wonder if she'd just woken, or if she has yet to sleep. Taking a quick step back, I right myself, pulling my shoulders back and wiping my eyes. She looks me over with a disinterested frown.

"Is she dead then?" she asks, her nasal voice haughty.

I know, because she is Rina's sister, I should have some sympathy for her, but I can't muster a single ounce. Nodding, I fight against the crushing weight inside my chest.

With one hand, she flips her hair off her bare shoulder. "I suppose I shouldn't be too upset. At least she's finally free of that facade of a marriage."

I feel my mouth open before I even decide to speak. "In case you've forgotten, it was your fault she was forced into that wedding."

She stares at me blandly. "In truth, I think we share the credit for that. You were, after all, the one whoring yourself out. All I did was report your actions to the empress." Her accusation draws me up short, mostly because she's not entirely wrong.

"That's rich, coming from my husband's whore," I say as calmly as I can manage.

She continues, ignoring my comment. "And, of course, I'll need to notify Father. He'll be sorely missing the income her husband was providing. But then, soon enough, he'll be receiving income from my husband—more than enough to cover his debts."

I should leave, I know it. But there's something in her tone that makes me sickly curious. "Why is that? Is Peter finally marrying you off to some lord or other in a valiant effort to repair your damaged reputation? Because I fear it is far too late for that, Elizavetta."

She snorts in a most unladylike manner. "Of course not. He's going to marry me."

It's all I can do not to laugh. "Oh? Taken to polygamy now, has he? Well, don't set your heart on it. You know well how fickle Peter's attentions can be. Soon, he'll be crowned, and I along with him. Whatever shallow promises he may make to get under your skirts, remember that he is married to *me*."

She steps close, far too close, near enough that I feel her wine-bitter breath on my face when she speaks, her expression one of disdain. "Peter loves me. I have always been loyal to him, unlike you. Soon, he will have all the power he needs to finally divorce you and put me in your place, as his one true wife and empress."

I feel my ire rise and step forward, forcing her to back up just a fraction. "Don't think for a moment to threaten me. I am Peter's wife in the eyes of God and Russia, and I will not be removed so easily." My voice is tight as wound thread, ready to snap.

She glances from me to Alexander, who stands with his back against the wall, speaking in hushed tones to the archbishop, and then back to me. Her implication is clear.

"Your love is poison; can't you see that? To be loved by you means nothing but ruin and death. If only I'd known sooner, I could have warned my dear sister away from you. Every life you touch withers and dies. It's a good thing you never loved Peter. He's safe from you in that respect, at least."

My hands ball into fists, the tendons in my knuckles tugging at the joints. I have to force them open, have to force my voice to a manageable tone. "Have care how you speak to me, Elizavetta. I am the grand duchess and in every possible way, I am your better."

Her mouth twitches. "Your threats mean nothing. You will never be empress. Peter has promised me this. You will be set aside, and your brat will be illegitimated. Neither of you will ever sit upon the throne of Russia."

My hand is moving before I can stop myself. When it connects with the side of her face, the sound is sharp and the impact reverberates down my arm. She's thrown off balance and collapses to one knee.

I lean over her. "I *will* be empress and so help me, if you ever speak to me in such a way ever again, I will have you hanged for it. Be grateful for the scraps you are given, Elizavetta, and do not think to demand more. My patience with you died with your sister."

When she looks up at me, there is hatred in her eyes. I can only imagine the emotion is mirrored in my own.

Days turn into weeks, and I haven't left the seclusion of my room. Watching through my window as Rina's body is sent back to her family for burial, I realize numbness has set into my very bones. I'm tired. Tired of losing people I love. Tired of being in pain. But mostly, I'm tired of putting on a brave face. And despite the constant bustle of maids and ladies, of guests and guards, I can't help feeling very, very alone.

I lie in bed, watching dawn break and then dusk fall outside my window, losing myself in book after book, until finally, one night, I hear my outer door creak open. Sitting up, I expect one of my maids to come to tell me the empress has finally passed, or for Peter to stumble in drunk and angry about something or other. There is a light tap on the door to my private chamber instead.

"It's me. May I come in?" a masculine voice calls out.

I should not let this happen. I realize it even as I'm speaking, but there's no reason left in me. I'm clinging to the last shreds of myself, every new wound forming permanent scars on my heart. Rina's passing being only the freshest, rawest of them all. As much as I know he should not be here, I also can't help the flicker of hope that his arrival brings. The hope that, for at least a brief moment, I might not feel so terribly forlorn.

"Come in, Alexander."

Chapter
TWO

He pushes the door open and steps inside, flickering lamp in hand. He's in his black suit. Between that, his dark hair, and the deep shadows of the night, he's like a phantom in my presence—more ghost than physical man.

"I just needed to see you," he begins. "Needed to see that you were all right. It's been weeks."

I nod and he sets the lamp down, taking a seat on the chaise at the end of my bed, turning his body to look at me. I should be embarrassed, him seeing me in my nightclothes, but I'm not. We know each other far too well to pretend otherwise. He had, after all, been my first love, very nearly my husband, once.

In another lifetime.

"I can't seem to let her go," I say honestly. There's so much—so much love and guilt and hatred all wrapped together in knots, impossible to untangle and release. Our lives had been so irrevocably tied up in each other for so long. "I didn't realize how much I needed her, how much I loved her. Now I feel the absence of her everywhere."

He nods, dropping his eyes to the floor. "I can't help thinking that if I'd just stayed in Denmark. If I had refused to come back when the empress summoned me. She would still be here."

I shake my head. "You can't think like that."

He sighs. It's heavy and dry, like he's releasing a breath he's been holding for years. "I tried to do my best by her, tried to make her happy. But I never really could. You asked me to love her, and I did, for your sake at first, then later because it was impossible not to."

The first errant tear escapes my eye, and I determinedly wipe it away.

Despite everything, she found joy in her life, in a forced marriage to a man who loved another, in leaving her home and family behind for foreign lands. I can't help but wish I had half her strength. "She was happy; she told me so. She loved you— loved us both. She wanted you to know that it was enough. *You* were enough."

He nods, looking away. "And my son will never know his mother. He will never remember her face or know the songs she sang to him."

Crawling forward, I rest my hand atop of his. "Then you will have to tell him. Help him remember that his mother was good, kind, and strong. You tell him she loved him more than life itself."

His gaze swings back to me. "I will. We both will."

I force a smile and nod. "We will."

When he stands to leave, I feel my heart sink just a little, and I'm not altogether sure why. Maybe it's my grief, or my emptiness, but the idea of being alone again is nearly unbearable. The idea of him walking out that door…

I take a slow breath, even as my heart picks up its pace, beating so hard against my chest that I'm sure he can hear it.

Sergei was right. Alexander is dangerous to me, probably more dangerous than any empress, or duke, or war, or illness ever could be. Because in that moment, seeing him standing at my door, all the old feelings come flooding back. Suddenly, I'm fifteen again, drowning in his embrace. And some infinite, treasonous part of me relishes the fear.

I push the memory aside, clamping my mouth firmly shut before I can do something I know I will regret.

He looks at me over his shoulder, his dark eyes locked on mine, his expression like a raging tempest. When his lips part, my heart stills, waiting.

"Ask me to stay," he whispers.

I blink, my chest clenching painfully to remind me to take a breath. But I can't. Can't move. I can't think. Can't speak.

He turns fully toward me, taking one cautious

step forward. "Please." His voice is stretched thin like a pulled ribbon. "Ask me to stay."

I should send him away. Some small, far-off voice in my head chastises me for even hesitating. But I can't force the words from my throat.

Slowly, he reaches into his breast pocket and draws out a folded piece of parchment. Carefully unfolding it, he reads it aloud. "Paris. The day is long, and I weary of this place. Would that I could be born again, that I might once more touch your face. Though you are far and I am here, I miss you still, my love, my dear. Helen."

I swallow. My own words, left so carefully tucked into the pages of our secret book, so very long ago. If I'd known he would go back, that he would find my letter, I would not have left it there. But he did go back. And now my own words threaten to betray me.

"If you do not love me still, why leave this?" he asks, refolding the letter and tucking it away.

"It was a long time ago," I say weakly. "Sergei…"

Alexander shakes his head, raking his hand through his ebony hair in a frustrated gesture. "He's not here. He's gone. He left you here, alone in this place with no one to protect you. With no one to love you, except me."

I open my mouth to protest, to remind him that it was the empress who forced him from my side, but he holds up a finger.

"No, I know you love him, truly. And I know he cares for you as well. But you are not his wife, or his property. If you fear that loving me—admitting you love me—somehow makes you disloyal..." He smirks. "Well, just remember that I loved you first. And I will go to my end loving you all the same."

As his words settle in, I can't help but wonder if he's right. Can you love two people at once? Is such a thing even possible?

"It feels wrong," I say, shaking my head. A betrayal of two people I love so deeply, both gone now.

He crosses the room in three long strides, cupping my cheek in his palm. "Perhaps I don't know right from wrong anymore," he says. "Mayhap all that is left in me is need. Selfish, twisting desire. But I can't bear to face this night alone. I can't abide the thought of leaving this room and never again touching your face. I can't endure losing you. Not again."

He lowers his face to kiss me, but I turn away at the last minute. Everything in my head is running together like wet paint on a canvas. A blur of colors and emotions. Loneliness and longing, lust and tenderness, all wrapped up in a mess of brushstrokes.

I close my eyes, trying to force the world to hold steady once more.

With a touch so light I scarcely feel it at first, he touches his fingertip to my elbow, slowly drawing it up my arm, taking my sleeve up with it. When he reaches my shoulder, he brushes over the fabric to the exposed skin of my neck, gently drawing the nightdress off my shoulder. A chill breaks out across my flesh. Even now, I'm helpless against his caress. I try to remember how it felt, his fingers twisted in my hair, his lips scorching against my skin, but I find I can't quite bring it to mind. My body flushes, smoldering with the desire to feel all those things again.

"Does this feel wrong?" he asks, lowering himself onto the bed beside me. Before I can answer, his lips are tracing their way up my neck, finally stopping to kiss my jaw.

"Let me be your Paris once more," he begs.

And just like that, I'm undone. I'm not sure if it's love or desire or something more or less, but I can feel myself unspooling in his arms. It's just as overwhelming as the first time he kissed me, and somehow, the pull is stronger now. I know it's not the right thing. I know it's selfish, and stupid, and dangerous. But, in this moment, this second, I can't seem to force myself to care.

"Please don't," I whisper.

He draws back, his expression defeated. Then I wind my fingers into the hair at the nape of his neck, drawing him close enough that our noses touch.

"Please don't go," I say, unable to keep the trembling from my voice.

He moves forward so quickly that it steals my breath.

I'm not sure when he finally sneaks from my chamber, but when I open my eyes in the light of morning, he's gone. I roll over, searching for his scent on my pillows to confirm it hadn't just been a dream. Instead, I a find a small note tucked under the pillow.

Did my heart love 'til now? Forswear its sight. For I never saw true beauty 'til this night.

I nibble on the end of my thumb as I read the verse over and over, a silly grin spreading across my face. As soon as I feel my spirit lift, the guilt crashes in.

I'm not a child, to be helpless at his touch, nor a weakling to need him at my side. Still, my heart aches. It aches for the loss of my friend, for my far-away love, and for the empty bed beside me. Sitting upright, I run my fingers through my hair, carefully working out the knots as I go. I stare at the note a few more moments before scooping it up and crinkling it into a ball.

"This is madness," I chastise myself.

The door swings open and Dashka glides in, a maid behind her setting a tray of food on my bedside table.

"What's that, Your Grace?" she asks, cheerfully drawing back the curtains and letting the early light stream in.

The maid curtsies and leaves us. I pluck a roll from the tray. "Love. It is madness, don't you think?"

She sits beside me, her thin lips puckered. "I don't know much about love. My marriage was arranged when I was only thirteen. But yes, I imagine love is the height of insanity. It certainly drives people to do terrible things. Great things, too. But terrible things."

"Have you never been in love?" I ask, taking a bite.

She shrugs. "I love my husband, though it isn't as it appears in books or plays. It's a very sensible type of love. I love him for providing for me, for blessing me with his name and reputation. That's a kind of love, I suppose."

I take a bite, considering her words. It's true; respect and gratitude are forms of love. Is it so terribly wrong of me to want more? Could I allow myself to find happiness in solitude? I swallow, imagining myself whiling away my days, riding, reading, or perhaps shopping for new gowns, as so many of the other noble ladies do. Then I imagine retiring to my bed, cold and alone. No, I do not imagine I can exist without passion. Perhaps I could have once, but now that I've had a taste of it, there will be no going back for me. No matter how complicated it makes my life, I need passion like a man needs air. Or perhaps, I just want it badly enough that I refuse to do without it ever again.

"I cannot imagine a life without great passion. I think it would be far too long and tedious. Is that terribly selfish of me?"

She tilts her head. "You are the grand duchess. If anyone has a right to be selfish, it's you. The fact that you even wonder about it makes you better than most."

I feel my face fall. In my mind, I do not deserve such praise. "But how are you?" I ask, changing the subject.

She frowns. "Ekaterina's death has been very difficult. She was such a wonderful sister. Not like Elizavetta. Rina was always patient with me, always kind. I appreciate you letting me take her place as your maid of honor."

I take her hand. "She loved you so much. How could I not do the same? I see so much of her goodness inside of you."

She smiles. "And she loved you, as well. She used to send letters telling me all about the balls and the plays you attended together. But more often, she talked about how much she admired you. Respected your courage and your strength. To hear her speak, it was as if you were an angel sent from heaven itself."

Once more, a terrible guilt writhes inside of me. "I am no angel—far from it. I have done dreadful things, Dash. Made mistakes I will never be able to atone for, and I have allowed myself to be selfish in ways you might never understand." The bitter memory of sprinkling the poison in the empress' tea floats into my mind. I think of every lie I've told, of every misstep I've made. "I'm not proud of my choices, but neither would I retract a single one," I finally say.

"Sometimes, the only choices you have are horrible ones," she says. "But you must still choose. That is when you know you are strong, and there is grace in the struggle."

I glance at her, admiring her quiet fortitude. She is, in so many ways, like Rina. So wise for her years. Intelligent, kind, and good. "You are a good soul, Dashka. I wish I were as good."

She shakes her head. "Don't say that, Your Grace. You are a good soul as well. Not as innocent as or naive as I am, but good nevertheless. You will be a fine queen."

"I hope so," I mutter around another bite. There's a cup of what looks like midnight-black tea on the tray. I pick it up, examining the contents. It smells burnt somehow. "What on earth is this?"

She nods to it. "That's a new drink the cook thought you might enjoy. It's called coffee. It can be bitter, so there is cream you can add to it. She says it's all the rage at French Court."

"Coffee? Odd." I take a sip and nearly gag. It's strong, so much more bitter and heavy than tea, but, still... I take another sip. "It's quite good, I think." I say, admiring the warmth of the cup in my hand.

Dashka beams. "I thought you'd enjoy it."

As we begin the tedious process of dressing and grooming, I sip on the beverage, asking for a second cup soon after the first. Soon, my heart speeds up, my face flushes, and I feel more awake and alive than I've felt in weeks. I let my mind drift. Someday, sooner rather than later, I will be queen. What sort of queen do I want to be? I know I will have to decide. Will I be loyal? Faithful? Will I be kind or courageous? Will I be content sitting quietly, or will I stand boldly against those who oppose me?

Suddenly, things seem very clear.

"It's the coffee," Dashka says, smirking.

Somehow, I think it's more than just that.

Chapter THREE

"The empress is dead!" The deep, thunderous voice of the court herald echoes throughout the corridors of Oranienbaum Palace. Bells ring like heartbeats in the distance as the nation mourns the loss of their sovereign.

I sit in my chamber, drinking coffee with Dashka. Neither of us speak, but the emotion shared between us is one of relief—not grief. It's not a surprise. Only the day before I received word from Sergei, who had been recalled to St. Petersburg, telling me that her time was near. I had tossed the letter into the fire, uneasy knots forming in my belly at the thought of seeing him again. Our correspondence is now so rigid and formal, I wonder if we have any relationship at all. Add to that the fact that I've taken Alexander to my bed, and my emotions are awash with turmoil. But not about this. This news isn't a shock—she'd been clinging to life for far too long already—but there's a deep sense of calm that pervades my senses.

I take a sip, letting the bitter warmth fill my mouth. It's cold in Oranienbaum, the relentless gasp of winter clinging like frost to glass across the massive grounds. Outside my window, the snow falls. It's Christmas and there is cheer enough, though perhaps now, terrible as it is to think, I've gotten the only gift I ever really wanted. A life free of the empress and her scheming.

All I can think as I take another dainty sip of coffee is how much I hope she suffered, and how much I pray she knows now, finally, the part I played in her slow demise. My soul is forever scarred by my decision to steal her life, whether or not my attempt succeeded. And I will wear it as a badge of honor, a memorial of the first time I took my fate into my own hands. And even as I sit here, watching delicate white flakes sprinkle past my window, I know it will not be the last.

A tap at the door draws my attention, and I set the cup on the bone-white saucer. "Yes?" I say, my tone as relaxed as a freshly fed kitten.

My steward steps in, the feather protruding from his black cap waving as he bows. "Your Grace, His Imperial Highness requests your presence."

I nod gently and turn to Dashka. Her long, yellow hair is powdered nearly white, curled and mounded atop her head. Though we both despise the look, it is still the height of fashion, so we occasionally bow to it. Today, however, I'm feeling rebellious.

"Help me prepare," I order.

Calling in two additional maids, I dress in my midnight-black gown, my mother's onyx necklace dripping tear-shaped stones around my neck, and allow them to add my adornments: my royal-blue sash that marks my appointment to the Order of St. Catherine, my red and gold ribbons, a black lace veil, and finally, they hold up my gold and ruby tiara.

"You don't want us to dress your hair?" one nervous young maid asks.

"No," I firmly respond, glancing at my reflection in the ornate, gilded mirror. My skin is pale as milk, my lips stained red with berry juice, and my eyes rimmed in kohl. The overall contrast with my dark hair and dress produces a stunning effect. To powder my hair white would ruin it. Besides, every noble woman at court will be dressed in their widest panniers, with their white hair piled high atop their heads. To make a suitable impression, I must be... more.

They brush my hair back tight against my head and twist, fanning it at the back into an elaborate bun before finally setting the tiara upon my head.

Dashka sets the maids to their next task, packing my rooms for transportation to the Winter Palace, where Peter and I will now take up residence.

As I lead my entourage through the gilded halls of Oranienbaum, I allow my eyes to linger on every painting, bust, statue, and woven tapestry as we move toward the main staircase. This place has been as much my home as any place has ever been, and it is here that I finally managed to carve out some small measure of happiness for myself. It will be hard to leave it behind.

Even as Peter has grown more distant and reclusive, I've blossomed. The nobles often seek my council, and visiting guests and even key generals come to my chambers after dinner to drink, sing, and dance with myself and my ladies. Even the serfs who come to court seeking justice or assistance kneel at my feet. When Alexander drops in the procession behind me to my right, I offer him a hint of a smile.

Peter stands outside his door, his man Mikhail to his right and Jean-Luc, the captain of his guard, to his left. Two footmen wait in the rear, each holding a small box. I know all too well what they contain. One is a set of miniature soldiers that he refuses to be separated from since his hunting dogs got loose in his chamber and chewed the last set to splinters, and the other holds a blue uniform jacket with gold buttons. They bear the standard of Prussian royalty, the crowned black eagle grasping a scepter. I cling to the hope that I will be able to dissuade him from wearing it, as we are still in the throes of war with Prussia.

When Peter offers me his arm, there is a mischievous glint in his sky-blue eyes that I haven't seen for some time. He's been so worried that the empress, in her ever-worsening condition, would pass him over in succession in favor of my son that I doubt he's slept in weeks. But now, she can harm us, threaten us, and abuse us no more. Her passing isn't just a death—it's a liberation. All around us, church bells ring out, echoing through the air in dulcet tones, ordering any who can hear into solitary mourning.

But today is not a day of sorrow. Not for us.

It's a day of reckoning.

It's only a few hours ride but when the carriage pulls up on the edge of the river overlooking the massive fortress of Peter and Paul, it feels like days have passed. Peter is chatting excitedly about the celebration he has planned for his arrival back at Winter Palace. He's so enlivened that I genuinely feel bad when I have to chastise him, gently reminding him that during the weeks of mourning, while the empress' body is on public display, we must at least pretend to grieve her loss. The funeral arrangements—especially for a monarch—are intricate, steeped in tradition, and, in Peter's mind, unbearably long and dull. With a shrug, he finally agrees to postpone it, but he is quite adamant we find the traveling acrobats that preformed summers last at

Paul's blessing feast.

The feast I missed in my extended confinement, at the empress' orders of course.

I agree with him, swallowing back my residual bitterness.

Leaving the carriages behind, we walk in procession across the Ioannovsky Bridge and into the heart of the island, where the city garrison and members of the Holy Synod await us outside the grand cathedral. I stand in awe of it, unable to keep my eyes from tracing their way up the tall, golden spire and fixing them on the golden angel atop. Of course, I've seen it several times from the opposite bank of the Neva river where Winter Palace sits perched not far from the sandy beach, but up close, it's absolutely breathtaking in its stark simplicity. It's as if the structure itself holds its breath, watching Peter and I as we approach, silently judging our worth.

Once inside, the humble exterior gives way to decadent and lavish gilding, massive frescos and stained glass reaching the highest walls. Peter leads our small procession into the cathedral, passing under the giant, golden iconostas that arches above us and into the bell tower, pausing in front of the Archbishop of Novgorod, who stands solemn in his long, white robes. His face is pruned with age and his are eyes small and sharp like those of a wary mouse. His beard is long and more white than black.

When Peter approaches, the archbishop kneels,

his hands rising and offering a prayer to the heavens in gratitude for our safe arrival. The ceremony is hastily preformed—at Peter's insistence. It's no secret that Peter prefers a more Protestant faith, and he has little patience for the drawn-out pomp and ceremony of the Orthodox ways. Mikhail has to whisper in his ear twice to prompt Peter to recite his lines, and he yawns twice, both times in jest, making the rest of the priests shift nervously. Finally, the archbishop blesses Peter, crowning him the official head of the senate, reigning monarch, and gosudar. It's a placeholder crown, the formal coronation will have to wait until after the funeral, but Peter wastes no time demanding everyone present give him their oath and kneel before him. We all drop to one knee on the cold, marble floor. Out of the corner of my eye, I see, all lined in a row, the tombs of past monarchs, realizing that one day, this stunning cathedral will host my eternal rest as well. A shiver drives up my spine and into the back of my neck so hard I have to clench my eyes shut against it. More prayers are offered, paperwork is signed and sealed, and it's done.

Peter is king.

When I finally stand, I realize the Archbishop of Novgorod is staring at me, even as Peter boisterously turns his back on the man, waving for his valet to hand him one of the boxes. Retrieving the Prussian uniform, he quickly puts it on, his valet buttoning it with swift fingers before stepping back and bowing reverently. I open my mouth to speak, but before I can say anything, Peter turns to me and smirks.

"Farewell, little mother. I shall see you at supper." And with that, he strides out the central doors, earning him a look of stern reproach from the other bishops in attendance and leaving me dumbfounded.

With a horse and a handful of guards, Peter rides ahead to Palace Square to meet the remaining gentry, lords, and of course, the townsfolk who have gathered to catch sight of their new emperor. Meanwhile, my guard Grigori Orloff and I remain behind. The archbishop turns to me, bowing deeply.

"Your Imperial Highness, may I speak with you for a moment?" he asks.

I nod and follow him toward the altar.

"These are delicate times," he begins softly. "And as empress consort, yours is now a heavy responsibility. His Highness will need all the care and tenderness a wife can provide, but you must also offer wise counsel, whenever you are able."

I feel myself laugh. "Are you suggesting that I run my husband?" I jokingly ask.

His face is stern beneath his long, gray beard. "Of course not. I only want you to know that I am here should you ever require guidance. And since His Highness refuses to attend mass, perhaps you might pass some of the wisdom you find along to him."

It's very clear what he's saying. He's afraid Peter's staunchly anti-orthodox sentiments will threaten the church. He's right to be afraid. Peter is widely known to detest the church, and with Protestant popularity growing in Europe—especially in Prussia—it's fair to think Peter will seek to extend it here.

"I will, as always, look to the wisdom you offer when I find myself in need of counsel, and I will, of course, pass that along to Peter. But I think you overestimate the weight my words carry with him."

He frowns. "If that is so, then I fear for us all."

His words are blunt, and I'm surprised to hear him be so frank with me. Of course, Peter's reputation on such matters is well known, but even so. I nod, doing my best to ease his worry with my expression, or to at least allow him to see that I take the matter seriously.

Drawing a small envelope from his robe, he extends his hand to me. "Her Majesty entrusted me with this letter for you before she died. I hope, for your sake, it brings you some comfort and wise counsel."

I slowly take the letter, as if it's a dangerous creature that must be handled carefully lest it turn and bite me. *She's gone*, I remind myself. There's nothing she, or her letters, can do to harm me now. Yet still, I'm gripped with fear.

"May I have a few moments alone to pray?" I ask. He nods, waving his hand toward a row of chairs by the altar before excusing himself with a deep bow.

Once it's only Grigori and me in the room, I tear open the familiar seal. I expect to see Elizabeth's wide, scrolling handwriting flowing across the page, but instead, it's tiny, each letter shakily inked, with splotches and smears betraying her fragile condition upon writing it.

Catherine,

There are many things I wish to say to you, but I fear my time grows short. I know things between us have been strained; I also know that you have hated me for the choices I've made. None of that matters now. Russia is fragile. It has been so since the death of my father, perhaps even before then. I knew when I chose Peter as my heir that he was broken. I thought I could mend him, at least enough to make him suitable to sit on the throne. I fear I have failed in that respect. Peter is an imbecile. The whole of Europe knows it. That's why I chose you, why I fought so hard to shape you into the person I need you to be—the person Russia needs you to be. For a time, I wasn't sure I succeeded. Then I tasted the poison you so carefully added to my tea.

Imagine my surprise to discover that, all this time, my kitten had claws of her own. It was then that I knew you could handle Peter, could handle anything that might be thrown your way. Peter may wear the crown, but there is a power inside you that cannot be denied. I saw a glimpse of it the first time we met. You reminded me so much of myself, so much of the person I was before I was thrust into taking the throne from Ivan. Circumstance is the oven in which we rise, and you have risen.

Perhaps that is what Sergei sees in you as well, your potential for greatness. He saw the same in me once, and he would have stood beside me against the world if I'd only allowed it. But I was too proud to accept him. I have thought for some time that love was weakness, that needing support from others means you are incapable of standing alone. It is only now, in these final hours, that I see how wrong I was about that. I'm going to die alone—surrounded by people, grieved by a nation, but truly loved by none.

My only consolations are that I chose well when I brought you to Russia. I know she will be safe in your hands, and that I will be remembered always, for my life's blood was shed for this nation, and history will not forget it.

HRM
Elizabeth

Rising, I return to my guard. We make our way to the carriages that will carry me back to Winter Palace, while I try to think of a time when I didn't hate my empress.

I busy myself with overseeing the details for that night's mourning feast, assigning rooms to our new household, appointing new positions with my personal staff, and helping make funeral arrangements. Its hours before Peter returns, his face flushed, absolutely exuberant.

"I had no idea how much they adored me," he says, pacing the room as if unable to hold himself still.

I sit, sipping on a cup of tea. "That's wonderful."

"No, you don't understand. There were hundreds—no, thousands—of people—lords and peasants and soldiers. They all pushed and scraped just to catch a glimpse of me. And when I stood on the platform, they all cheered. As one, they shouted and fell to their knees. They are absolute in their devotion for me," he says, sounding as surprised as I feel.

It's true that the assembly was made mostly of nobles and landowners, all of whom could be counted on to pledge themselves to whatever monarch happened to be next in line, but to hear Peter tell it, he had the genuine love of the people. And that surprised me. Many of those same people had been vying only weeks before for Elizabeth to remove Peter from the line of succession altogether. And him showing up in that blasted Prussian uniform shouldn't have won him any praise either. In the doorway, Peter's man Mikhail stands stoic, his face unreadable.

I listen as Peter goes on and on, though my mind is occupied by the hundreds of details we must now attend to. As if my concern is a beacon in the night, Sergei Salkov and Grand Chancellor Count Bestuzhev sweep into the room with a handful of diplomats and senators in their wake. They each drop to one knee before the new emperor, who pauses from his incessant jabbering just long enough to greet them.

Bestuzhev steps forward, a book of documents tucked under his arm. "Your Highness, if you have a moment, I would like to discuss the new appointments."

Peter waves for the man to sit, but he resumes pacing, nearly dancing really, around the room, humming to himself.

"First, we would like to inform Your Highness of the current diplomats in residence," he begins, but I cut him off, setting my teacup back in its saucer. It's all I have not to lock eyes with Sergei, though I can feel him staring at me as if the heat of his gaze could light my dress aflame. But I cannot allow myself the distraction now—that will have to wait.

"In residence, we host ambassadors from France and Austria, our allies Count Mercy and Baron de Breteuil, as well as Lord Alexander Mananov, who is the current Swiss ambassador, returned with us from Oranienbaum Palace. Is that correct?" I ask.

He nods, beginning to name all the lords, advisors, senators, and chancellors. I know each name on his impressive list. Peter, however, has probably retained very little. That's all right; all the better for me if he needs me to help remind him.

"And, of course, I serve as grand chancellor," Bestuzhev finally says.

Peter turns on his heel, leveling a glance at him. "For now."

I've never seen the old man move with quite so much speed as when he snaps to his feet. "Your Highness?"

"I'm disbanding my aunt's former cabinet, of course. I will keep a few, but I have already sent for many replacements," Peter announces, spinning back to the window and looking out. "It is a new era for Russia. And I will begin it surrounded by men I can trust."

Bestuzhev glances my way nervously, but I can only shrug. The bad blood between them runs deep, since my arrival when Bestuzhev poisoned me to prevent the treaty with Prussia, which had failed on every account. Peter had delivered swift, painful retribution on my behalf, and to this day, Bestuzhev bore the scars of that torture. As for me, I moved past it long ago, realizing that Bestuzhev could be as powerful an ally as he once had been an enemy. Peter, however, never forgives a slight. To the left, I see Mikhail in the doorway, his expression proud. No doubt, he will take the role of grand chancellor.

None have been more loyal to Peter, including me.

"And your private staff?" I ask Peter, who is now pretending to fence with an invisible partner.

He waves me off. "Appoint who you will, little mother. I have more pressing matters."

I stand. "Lord Salkov, Count Bestuzhev, if you will join me in the study, we can tend to these tedious matters for His Highness while he prepares for the funeral banquet tonight."

For the first time, I allow myself to look Sergei fully in the face. My heart skips in my chest. He is as handsome as ever, even if he does look a bit tired. His dark hair is tussled and his blue-green eyes are set deep, like sea glass set in stone. There is the ever-present hint of hair just along his jaw, making his face look even more chiseled. As with Alexander, I feel myself pulled toward him by an unseen force. As if no time has passed at all, the urge to throw myself in his arms is driving me forward. It's my will alone that holds me still as I pass, leading them both to the study.

Settling in at the empty desk, I send the maid for wine and biscuits.

Sergei sits on the lounge across the room as Bestuzhev and I begin the task of assigning new posts.

"Pierre Marcel is a French duke, a lecherous man who drinks too much and laughs too hard," he says, announcing the final candidate for Peter's chamber men.

I sit back. "Then I'm sure he and Peter will get along perfectly. Besides, another Frenchman will do Peter some good. He might be more willing to listen to advice from a man so much like himself."

"I respectfully disagree," he insists. "Sergei, what say you?"

Sergei speaks, his tone less than amused. "I say that she is the empress and will do as she pleases."

Bestuzhev sits back, as if now realizing for the first time that I, too, have power over him. The color fades from his cheeks. He may have been Elizabeth's favorite, but he will find no such favor in the new Imperial Court.

"Of course, as you say, Your Highness."

He gathers up his papers and bows, taking his leave. Without a word, Grigori, my guard and ever-present shadow, peeks his head in, nods, and shuts the door, leaving Sergei and me completely alone.

When he stands, I expect him to cross the room and lift me into his arms as he once had, but instead, he drops to one knee, his fist over his heart.

"Your Highness," he begins slowly. "I am deeply sorry for not returning to your side sooner."

I fold my hands in front of me. "Then what kept you away?" I ask softly. No matter his answer, I know it will change nothing in my heart.

"The empress, she was gravely ill, and demanded I send edicts to our allies regarding the movement of troops into Berlin. Then she summoned me back to be at her side when she passed. I arrived only days ago."

I sigh. Of course. It would be her last dying effort to keep Sergei away from me. I knew as much, but I needed to hear him say the words, to tell me he would have rather been at my side.

"When I heard Rina died, I went to the library and found your book of poems, the one you used to read so often. I sent it to the palace anonymously, hoping you would know it was from me and that it might bring you comfort." He stands. "I wanted nothing more than to be at your side, but our forces were so close to ending this war. I knew that if the empress passed, Peter would recall the troops and it would all have been for nothing. I only tried to keep her alive as long as possible."

I swallow the dry lump in my throat. He sent the book? That's how Alexander had come across it? I stare at him, wondering if he has any idea about the letter it contained. "I missed you," I say, my voice barely a whisper.

"And I missed you, deeply," he says, his voice tight.

"Well, are you just going to stand there or are you going to kiss me?" I demand, smiling. "Or do I have to order you to? I am empress now—"

He's holding me before I can finish the sentence.

His arms coil around my waist, tightening as he crushes his lips against mine, desperate at first, and then softer, more like breathing rather than struggling. He relaxes against me, and I feel his hands slide up my back and into my hair. I exhale into his mouth, playfully nibbling at his bottom lip. He groans, and a flush warms my face.

"I wasn't sure you would still want me," he murmurs into my hair as he holds me close. "I didn't want to presume."

I pull back so he can see my face. "I will always want you. Many things have changed, but never that." I pause, knowing there will be no right time for the truth I must share. As I open my mouth to utter the painful words, he stops me, pressing a finger against my lips.

"It doesn't matter."

"What doesn't matter?"

He smiles sadly. "Whatever you want to say that put that look on your face. Nothing matters except that you are here now, and you love me still. That is all I need to know."

I shake my head, but he kisses me again. He kisses me until everything else fades away.

Chapter

FOUR

T hat night, the banquet is somber, no boisterous laughter—other than Peter's, of course—with no music, no dancing, and no jokes. Each noble is formally introduced by the herald, and they take turns bowing and kissing Peter's hand. They chat with me about everything from news that the Russian Army has taken Berlin to spice trades with the Indies. People take turns saluting the fallen empress and the new emperor. They even raise a glass to me.

"A toast to our lovely new empress, Her Majesty Catherine, may her reign be long and prosperous," Count Mercy says in broken Russian. I smile, despite the faux pas. It's Peter's reign, after all. I glance over to see if he's taken notice, but he's much too busy chatting with Mikhail.

When the feast ends, Peter hurries off to his new chamber, no doubt eager to meet his mistress. I have to practically run to catch him in the hall. Though our rooms are in the same wing, I am far down the corridor from him. He has chosen to take up Elizabeth's old rooms, the sprawling, five-chamber area set aside for the reigning monarch. I don't imagine all the gold, jewels, and silk in the world could make me want to lie in that bed—with or without Peter. So I stay close enough not to amass much gossip, but far enough not to have to see him if I choose not to.

"Peter," I call out.

He stops mid-step, looking at me quizzically. "Yes?"

"I was hoping I might accompany you to your rooms," I say lightly. "I've not seen you much of late, and I'd like to catch up. To talk about our plans for the future."

He nods and offers me his arm. Thank heavens he hasn't drank enough to let his good mood sour, at least not yet.

I have to admit, his outer chamber is breathtakingly beautiful. Everything is gold and green—a change made at his request—with thick tapestries woven with strands of gold and silver that hang along the walls. There are tables with statues of hunting dogs and busts of heroic warriors like Alexander the Great, and his own namesake as well. I settle myself onto the settee as he calls for a tray of brandy.

"It's been quite an exciting day for you, hasn't it?" I ask, picking up one of his toy soldiers from the open box on the table and examining it. Slowly, I set it down on the table, facing Peter. He smirks, retrieving a toy of his own and setting it facing mine in a miniature standoff.

"It has been glorious. If I had known how much my people loved me, how much they needed me, I would have slit her throat years ago."

He's talking about Elizabeth, of course. How ironic that I so often had to talk him out of killing her, only to later poison her myself.

Fate, it seems, makes fools of us all.

"Well, you have the throne now and she is gone. Have you thought about what you want to do first?"

He takes another wooden soldier from the box, adjusting its hat carefully, setting it to face me. I do the same.

"I am going to end the war. I'm already having Bestuzhev draft up a treaty with Prussia. Tomorrow, I'm ordering the troops out of Berlin."

I swallow, moving another soldier. "Are you sure that's what you want to do? Prussia is all but defeated. They can't stand against us much longer. We could win the war outright, and then approach Prussia with a treaty. You would certainly be able to command better terms, and you would retain France and Austria as allies as well."

He shakes his head. "No. Frederick sent me a letter only last week. His forces are overrun. He will be destroyed if we don't pull back. He appealed to me as a friend and a fellow ruler. I will not see him decimated for the sake of Austria." He stops, picking up a soldier and pointing it at me. "Do you disagree?"

I take a long breath. Truly, I don't. Prussia was my home once, and I want to secure peace as much as anyone. But I would not endanger current allies to do it. Still, Peter has made his mind up and to push the point will only drive a wedge between us.

"No, of course not. I support your decisions, whatever they may be," I say with a nod of my head.

He smiles, setting his soldier with the others.

"I would offer a few words for you to consider on other matters, if you would hear them," I say, slowly turning each soldier I've laid down so they are facing me, in unison with his own wooden army.

"Of course." He rocks back on his heels, standing when the tray of brandy is delivered only long enough to pour us each a glass, waving off the footman who tries to do it for him. When he holds it out to me, I take it without touching his fingers. The last thing I want is to give him any wrong impressions about my intent tonight.

"Well," I say, taking a sip. "The people of the village love you—that much is obvious. We might extend that goodwill a bit by making some minor policy changes."

"Such as?"

"Well, the salt tax for one. You could lower it just

a bit; that would give the serfs some relief. Times have been very difficult since the fevers and the pox swept the country. A small measure of relief would show how concerned and benevolent you are."

He nods. "Yes, that is a good idea."

"And as for the lords, you could abolish the mandatory service law. That would go a long way to keeping them in your good graces, as well as ensuring that young nobles would be in your debt."

He salutes me with his glass. "All wonderful ideas, little mother. And I have also been thinking of reforming some of the church practices."

I pause, taking a drink to hide my concern. "Which practices?" I ask after swallowing.

"I don't know. Maybe we can make them all shave off their beards and wear women's stockings!" He laughs, and I force a chuckle. "Better yet, I will seize all the church lands and property for the crown. Make them beg in the streets like paupers."

The shock of his words hits me like ice water. If he does that, it will destroy the core of the church, turn it and those who hold firm to its doctrine against us. My mind spins, looking for an alternative. I force a smile.

"You know what would be worse than that? If you allowed some of the exiled Protestant leaders back into Russia. That would drive them mad! They have worked so hard to keep them from moving into Russia. I mean, can you imagine? If Russia was seen as the champion for religious tolerance in Europe?" I force another laugh.

This time, he doesn't join me. His face is blank as he tries to decide if it's a viable idea.

"Oh, no, Peter. You mustn't. The clergy would have absolute fits," I add, hoping it will push him toward the idea rather than away from it. It would be a small consolation, returning those exiled, but better that than the alternative.

"That's a wonderful idea. It would serve them right," he says finally.

I nod. "As you say."

A knock at his chamber doors draws his attention away from me. His valet steps in and announces his late-night visitor. "Lady Elizavetta Vorontsova, Your Highness."

Peter waves his hand.

Elizavetta bounces merrily into the room, her bright red curls bobbing as she moves. That is, until she catches sight of me. She freezes, her face settling into an expression of shock and rage. I almost feel bad for her.

Almost.

Peter hurries to her side, kissing her quickly on the cheek. "Hello, darling. Please, wait for me in the far chamber."

She nods, her mouth set in a thin line, and brushes past me to the rear chamber where Peter's private apartment sits. She slams the door behind her, and Peter smirks.

"A little envy is good for her," he says.

I frown but say nothing.

"I suppose you should go." His tone brightens as he adds, "Unless you'd like to stay. Oh, wouldn't that be interesting?"

My eyes widen before I can stop them, a horrified look stamping itself across my face. When he laughs, I curtsy and move to leave. He stops me with a hand on my elbow.

"Thank you for your counsel. And your friendship," he says.

These words are almost more shocking than the last, but I hide my surprise this time, achieving a look I hope is one of humility and meekness as I nod and take my leave of him. As soon as I'm out the door, I hear Elizavetta start shouting, and as much as I deplore them both, it brings a smile to my face. Grigori waits patiently for me to move.

"Is everything all right, Your Highness?"

I nod. His concern is touching, but unnecessary. He follows me down to my chamber where my maids wait to help me undress. I pause outside my door, looking at my handsome young guard. "Grigori, I am very tired. Please see to it that I have no visitors for the rest of the evening."

"None?" he asks.

"None."

When I'm finally alone in my bed, I think of

Sergei and Alexander. What a sad, fickle creature a woman's heart is. Yet, here I am. In love with two men, neither of them my husband. And I wonder if they will ever forgive me.

When I finally fall asleep, I dream of the green hills of Prussia, of doors opening and closing with the wind, and I'm not altogether certain why.

Chapter

FIVE

The next day, the morning light streams in from the large window in my room, the smell of fresh bread and sausage drifting up from the kitchens. I hear the maids bustling about, and I sit up in bed. There's a bell on my nightstand, and I ring it. Two maids come hurrying in. They dress me quickly and lead me to my bathing chamber where a dark-haired man waits. He reminds me a bit of Baron de Breteuil, all slender and tidy. When he speaks, I understand the resemblance.

"Your Highness, I am Jean-Michelle, your new hairdresser," he announces in French.

I nod. Of course. The Frenchmen had been Elizabeth's hairdresser, and now he is mine. It's the first time I've had a male hairdresser, but they are all the rage in Paris. Perhaps it's just another way the French are tossing aside conventional moral standards. The whole thing smacks of impropriety, and I can only imagine what my mother might say. Yet something about it feels decadent, rebellious. So when he was offered to me, I seized the opportunity.

"Please, have a seat and we will begin."

Unlike when Rina or Dashka did my hair, Jean is grueling, pulling, tugging, and teasing until my hair is as tall as he can make it. A small, stuffed bird is added to one side and three long curls hang down the back of my neck. He doesn't powder it, but leaves it rich and ebony.

It looks beautiful, but it feels like my neck might snap from the weight.

"Here, allow me," he says, wrapping a thick ribbon around my neck. Or at least it looks like a ribbon. But inside, it clearly has bones like a corset and in the back, two long spikes go up and into the back of my hair, supporting the weight just enough.

"Oh my," I say, admiring it.

He adds my crown and steps back, clapping excitedly. "Voila!"

I glance over my shoulder at Dashka, who is working on some needlepoint. "What do you think, Dash?"

She looks up and smiles. "You look lovely. Tomorrow, all the noble ladies will show up with birds in their hair, just you wait and see."

I grin. "What is on the schedule today?" I ask.

She picks up my small notebook from the table and hands it over to me to read. "Ah, a formal breakfast with the gentry, and then we hold open court. We are to receive the last of the nobles who have traveled in, and then we will finalize the state funeral plans. Oh, and I must do something about the gardens; they are in terrible shape. Can you send me the gardener after lunch?"

She curtsies. "Of course. And these came for you this morning."

She hands me two notes, both sealed in deep red wax. I hesitantly take them, feeling a flush crawl its way into my face. With a quick gesture, she ushers everyone else from the room. "Would you like me to go as well? I can give you a moment if..."

I move to the large settee, patting the seat beside me. "No, stay. You might as well know about all this. As my maid of honor, there are things you will know, things I will require you never to speak of. I've made quite a mess for myself, you see." I hold the letters to my lips, taking a deep breath. "Rina knew. She kept my secrets for many years. May I count on you to do the same?" I ask, already knowing the answer. She's young, and in the grasp of a nearly reverent devotion to me.

When she responds, her eyes are wide with sincerity. "Of course you can, Your Highness."

I pat the seat again, and she sits down. "You see, when I arrived at court, I fell in love with a man," I begin.

"Peter?" she asks.

I shake my head, smiling sadly. "No, not Peter. Though not for lack of effort. Peter has always been...

a difficult person to love. No, his name was Alexander." I pause, letting that sink in. She had known him only as her sister's husband, and the revelation must come as quite a shock to her because a small gasp escapes her lips.

I continue. "We were deeply in love. Secretly, we planned to run away together. However, the empress found out and forced him to marry Rina to keep us from each other. And it worked. But then I fell in love again. With Sergei. I've been having an affair with him since the wedding. Peter wouldn't have me, you see, after he found out I'd nearly run away with Alexander. He threatened to refuse me until he could have me declared barren and sent away. He was quite cruel. I found myself very alone, and Sergei... The love I felt for him as a friend became something much more. But when Rina died, I was so heartbroken. Sergei was gone, I was grieving, and..."

"You had an affair with Alexander?" she guesses, no judgment in her tone.

I nod. "You see, I love him still. I love them both. And I have no idea what I'm going to do. I know that I will tell them both the truth—I couldn't bear to lie to them—but what then? How can I possibly choose?"

Dashka takes a deep breath, smoothing her hands down her skirts before speaking. "I don't know much about love, or passion. But I do know what it means to be empress. I served as Elizabeth's maid for years as a girl. I saw her take lover after lover, and no one thought anything about it."

I smirk. "Oh, we thought a great many things about it."

She shakes her head. "What I mean is that it didn't lessen her—as a ruler or as a woman. She wasn't weaker for it. If anything, that she had the courage to act as a male king would have earned her some measure of respect. And peace. I believe she was, in that respect at least, quite content."

Thinking back to her letter, I wonder if that's a fair statement. Something dawns on me. "Were you here, when Sergei and the empress were lovers?"

My question surprises her. I can see it in her eyes before she looks away, nodding.

"What happened between them? Do you know? Will you tell me? Please, be honest," I beg.

She straightens in her seat. "It was midsummer. I remember because I thought it so odd that the fire had been lit when the whole palace was sweltering. Then I realized the empress had been burning clothes. I asked her about it, and she said that anything he'd given her, anything he'd touched, was soiled and she had to be rid of it. That is all I know. After that, he was gone for a time, but he returned to court a few months before you arrived I believe."

Realizing I'm picking at my bottom lip with my thumb, I drop my hands into my lap. "Thank you for your honesty," I say, holding up the letters. Not that it changes anything, but it does make me curious, and I'm not certain what drives it.

As I tear into the first letter, there's no doubt who it's from.

My dearest Helen,

I have kept my distance these weeks, as you have asked, but I long to be near you again. It pains me to see you walking down the hall, to hear your laugh in the distance. My arms yearn to hold you once more. Consent to meet me, to drive this darkness from my heart. You are, and have always been, the sunlight in my soul.

-Paris

I set the note aside, carefully opening the next. It's much more formal, the wide, scrawling letters practically etched into the paper with the force from which it was written.

Your Imperial Majesty,

Please forgive the informal nature of this letter. I have urgent matters, matters of some delicacy, of which I should like to discuss. If you are willing, please send for me at your earliest convenience.

Your humble and loyal servant,

General Sergei Salkov

I sigh, my heart feeling heavy as a stone in my chest. "To choose between them would mean losing one. And I simply cannot bear the thought," I admit in a cheerless whisper.

"Then there is only one choice, Your Majesty." I look up to see Dashka's face, her expression uncharacteristically stern. "And that is simply not to choose at all."

As her words roll through my mind, I cannot help but wonder if I have the courage for such a thing. Because to choose will mean losing one, refusing to choose might well drive them both from me. It's a terrible risk to take.

I feel her move to take my hand, and then hesitate. Being empress means no others are supposed to touch me without permission. I bridge the gap between us, gently patting her hand. Her expression is fierce, like a mother cat protecting her cub, and I can't help but smile at her gentle ferocity. "Don't fret on my account, Dash. I'm queen, after all. Ruler of Russia, if not of my own heart. And I will not falter, in this or anything else."

She smiles, relaxing back into the pale blue gown that threatens, by sheer size, to overtake her small frame.

The days pass quickly, three gone before I can

find a moment to take a single breath, or so it seems. I push through each new task like someone sleep-walking, always fully engaged in the minute details, using them as a distraction, keeping my mind far from other thoughts. The funeral is prepared, Peter's new laws are to be presented to the senate the following day, and as Dash predicted, the ladies of court have taken to mimicking my fashions with each new day. I have my first chance to see my son, and what a handsome little boy he's becoming. His hair is lighter than I expect, the patchy, dark hair he was born with having mostly rubbed off, replaced with soft, corn-silk strands, his eyes still blue as sapphires. He's fast despite his short legs, and he growls in frustration, throwing his wooden horse when one of the maids tries to clean up a pile of abandoned blocks in the corner. The nurses let me play with him only a short time before insisting he go back to the warmth of the nursery, for fear that he will fall ill. Still, it is enough. And I know there will be nothing keeping me from him now.

When I wake on the fourth day, I have a pounding in my head that rivals anything I've ever felt before. I manage to convince Jean to arrange my hair in a low, elegant, braided bun, citing the need to add a veil, which he elaborately cuts from a piece of black lace and tucks into my hair with expert fingers. He winds a delicate cord around the bun and lets it trail down the back of my neck before carefully settling my crown on top of my head.

"I will be making my way to the cathedral in a carriage with Peter," I inform my guard as I slip on my black satin elbow gloves. "He will return straightaway, stopping in the palace square to make a formal announcement of mourning, and then coming right back here. I will remain at the viewing to greet the mourners. Please see to it that a small contingent of guards remains behind. Peter will want his Holstein troops with him, no doubt." Grigori bows deeply and turns to make the arrangements while Dashka sits across from me, waiting to help me with my official sash and ribbons.

I try to remain stoic. It is a day of national mourning, after all, but there is an excitement inside myself that I cannot seem to stomp down. The new household is finally in order, and while Peter has been keeping himself at a distance since our first night back, he seems genuinely content for the first time that I can recall. Tomorrow, our new legislation will be signed. I took it upon myself to speak to the lords about the changes, and they all seem genuinely pleased. As if that weren't enough, I received a note from Peter that he has asked someone to join us at court that he thinks will please me. I cannot help but hope he has invited my dear brother, and with his desire to end the war between our nations, it would be a clever move, politically. I feel the flush in my cheeks just imagining it. I haven't seen him in so very long.

"You're smiling again," Dash whispers.

I pull my face slack once more.

Peter greets me at the top of the formal staircase. As I approach, I see him as I once had, as a young, vibrant man surrounded by his gentlemen of the chamber, Alexander and Mikhail, and his guards. Our eyes meet for the briefest second before his attention turns away. Though he's older now, his face partially scarred from the pox, his golden curls are just the same. My eyes slide past him to land on Alexander's face. He looks down and then back up, as if bowing with his eyes. His dark suit complements his naturally olive complexion and his dark, ebony black hair. I lift my chin as the herald formally announces us, stepping forward to accept Peter's now-outstretched arm.

The funeral procession is slow, and around us the world is bleak, the day gray and rainy. During the last part of the journey, Peter steps out, taking his place walking behind the casket. Every so often, he pauses, lagging behind so long the entire procession has to wait, and then he merrily jogs forward, smiling like an impish child. When he enters the carriage again at the bridge, he's winded. Though he doesn't speak to me on the journey, he stares out the window, waving eagerly to anyone and everyone as we pass. Finally, he slumps back into his seat, visibly distressed.

"What is it, Peter?" I ask, knowing well that despite appearances, neither of us is truly mourning this day.

He frowns petulantly. "I thought they'd be glad to see me. To know that they are in far better hands now. They should be celebrating!" he adds, slamming his palm against the carriage wall.

"People always grieve the passing of a monarch," I say, quickly adding, "no matter how much they were disliked in life. She belonged to them, and they have lost her. It's only natural to grieve such a loss, even when brighter prospects lay only on the horizon."

He shrugs but says no more. When we arrive at the cathedral, Peter steps out of the carriage and I follow. We should precede single file into the chapel, but Peter pauses, holding his arm out for me once again, drawing a cheer from the downtrodden assembly. This makes him grin. He waves to them, and I do the same. Once inside the doors, he releases my arm, taking the lead through another set of wooden doors, to the stone tomb where Elizabeth rests in a coffin of glass, just below the altar.

Though her face is covered with sheer, black gauze, I can make out her features perfectly. Even in death, she is lovely. Perhaps even more so, now that she is unable to inflict further harm or pain on my person. Glancing up at Peter, I see that his face has gone beet red. He's visibly shaking from head to toe as if at any moment he might burst out of his skin.

I turn to the guards and priests who wait behind us. "Please, give His Highness a moment to grieve, privately, before we begin the funerary viewing," I solemnly ask.

They bow and turn away, moving back to the doors. The archbishop pulls them closed a fraction of an instant before Peter explodes, pounding his fists against the glass.

"You callous, heartless, wicked bitch!" he screams. It echoes throughout the chamber and I pick up my skirts, rushing to his side.

"Peter, please," I say, grasping for his hands, but he pulls them away.

"No. She didn't deserve this." He waves his hand around the room. The tall candelabras are lit, chained pots of burning incense hang from the dais, and flowers litter the floor. "She was never fit to be ruler. Everyone knows she stole the throne from Ivan."

He's fully screaming and without thinking, I reach out and slap him, hard. The sound of it is like a clap of thunder. For a moment, he just stares at me.

"Peter, you must get a hold of yourself," I whisper sharply. "The lords and clergy are just behind that door. If they hear you speaking so, they may very well decide you are right and that the royal authority never laid with her, and thus, it doesn't lie with you either."

He blinks, his hand rubbing his reddened cheek. For a moment, I can feel my heart pounding like a hammer in my chest. When he moves, I twitch, expecting him to strike me back. But he doesn't.

"What makes you think of Ivan on this day?" I ask, trying to be gentle.

Looking back down at Elizabeth, he frowns. "She took him in the night; did you know that? She attacked him when he was only a helpless infant, and she threw him and his nurse in a dark cell for twenty-five years. If not for you, she probably would have done the same to me. She used to call me useless; did you know that? When I was young and my teachers would complain, she told them to beat me with the books if I refused to read them. How I hated her…"

"You are the true Romanov emperor, and you must not let anyone else think otherwise," I continue. He nods, looking back down at her waxen face. "And as far as Elizabeth, she will reap in death what she sowed in life; I am sure of that."

"I only wish I'd have done it myself," he muses quietly, a half smile spreading across his face.

I feel myself flinch at his words. "Better that you didn't. Better that your hands are clean."

When he looks up at me, it's like a knife slicing through me. I can feel him, peeling back my skin with only the power of his stare, exposing me for the hypocrite I so clearly am.

When he speaks, there's something wicked behind his words, a tone I cannot place, but it still manages to make me shiver. "Would you have killed her to save me? If she truly wanted to pass me over, would you have done it to keep me safe?"

I swallow. His question is too close to a confession for my comfort. Still, I cannot bring myself to lie. "For you, to secure your reign, I would."

"Because you love me?" he asks. I know I should say yes and profess my love, although it would be a lie, but I have no dishonesty in my heart just now.

"Because your fate and mine are bound. Perhaps they have been since the day we met as children. Whatever path we walk in this world, we must walk it together," I say.

He shakes his head. "You don't seem terribly happy about that."

I shrug. "If I've learned one thing, it's that happiness, true and lasting happiness, can only come from a place of trust."

"And you don't trust me?"

I raise one eyebrow, holding his gaze steady. "Should I?"

He says nothing, just inclines his head in my direction and strides from the room, throwing open the doors to the surprise of those beyond.

When he's gone, the archbishop joins me at the coffin. "You seem troubled, Your Highness. May I suggest the solace of confession?" he offers.

I shake my head, kneeling beside the coffin instead. "Thank you, but my soul is feeling far too confessed already," I say softly.

He nods and backs away. A line forms and the doors are thrown open to the waiting assembly, who form a quiet line and slowly proceed in. I remain on my knees as the mourners come and go, keeping my eyes closed in silent prayer. At some point, Grigori offers me a pillow for my knees, but I refuse it. The pain is good; it reminds me why I'm here, that this is my penance, my small atonement for the part I played in her death.

As I pray, I try to think of her as a young girl, born a princess but denied her legacy. She made some difficult choices, but she always remained strong and regal despite them. Perhaps that is what it means to be a ruler. Mayhap you have to sell off little pieces of your soul for the greater good. It's no wonder that she took so many lovers. I know all too well the hole those kinds of choices can make in your heart. Perchance she tried to fill it, however she was able. The longer I kneel, the more my heart opens for her, and the more I understand, until I feel the first of the tears slip from my closed eyes.

Finally, free of my hatred, I allow myself to grieve her passing.

I stand vigil beside her coffin for three more days, silently nodding as each person comes in, bids farewell to one empress, and bows before a new one. A few offer me tokens or items to place in the coffin. I always oblige, thanking them sweetly and offering what I hope is a reassuring smile.

Peter's new laws are passed quickly and even in the final hours of mourning, there is a collective sigh of relief visible in the faces of both serfs and nobles alike. They feared what sort of leader Peter would be, but he has passed the first hurtle.

That evening at dinner, I wear my best blue gown. Peter assures me I will want to look my best for our guest, and I am aflutter with excitement. Not only at the thought of seeing my dear brother again, but at the opportunity to meet with both Sergei and Alexander. Mourning has given me a great deal of time to reflect, and I have finally decided where my heart truly lies. Come what may, I will be better off for it, I think.

Though Peter is already seated, the crowd rises when I am announced. They raise their glasses to me even as they bow. I nod to the room and take my seat beside Peter. Elizavetta is on his right, in the place normally reserved for the chancellor, and I see that Bestuzhev has been relegated to a table near the rear of the room beside the French and Austri- an ambassadors; all three of them have their heads down, engaged in nervous chatter. I can't help but notice Peter is once again wearing the green uniform of the Prussian Army.

I open my mouth to question it but before I can, Peter stands, drawing the room into silence.

"My lords and ladies, it is my greatest pleasure to announce I have signed a treaty with King Fredrick. Our soldiers are being evacuated from Berlin as we speak. Thanks to my new Commandant of the Russian Army, Prince George Lewis."

Peter claps and others slowly, halfheartedly, join in. As for me, I'm too stunned to move. From the rear of the room, the doors open and George strides in, in a uniform matching Peter's.

The breath rushes from my lungs as if I've been kicked by a horse. My momentary disbelief is replaced by a flush of fear. I fight the urge to look at his face, keeping my eyes locked on the floor at his feet, as if seeing him will somehow solidify his presence.

My uncle. The man who had thought so carelessly to try to seduce me at only fourteen, the man I would have ended up married to had my marriage to Peter not succeeded. I swallow the bit of spiced lamb in my throat, but it refuses to go down, choking me. I take a drink of wine, and then another, before finally clearing it.

Peter stands from the table and greets him warmly, with a hug, as if they were brothers rather than great-uncle and nephew. George bows deeply and Peter laughs, draping an arm across his shoulders and leading him to the table. He quickly dismisses Mikhail with a wave and sets George in his place.

They begin talking in hushed tones. I can't quite make it out, but I have a deep, gnawing feeling that warns me off. Across the room, Count Mercy shoots me a concerned glance. He's very pretty for a man, slender features and a long, sloping nose. His hair is powdered and curled at the neck, his jacket adorned with the finest French lace at the neck and cuffs. His skin is so pale and without blemish that it matches the shade of white perfectly. Add to that his soot-black lashes that hide a pair of round, gray eyes, and he is a striking, though not imposing, figure of a man.

My eyes slide from him to Baron de Breteuil. In stark contrast, he's a tall, muscular man with a wide jaw and more rounded features. His hair is curled, though not powdered, and is dusty brown like old leather. He's staring at Peter as if he wished nothing more than to beat him with a stick. It's hard to blame him. By inviting George here, Peter is effectively throwing it in their faces that he intends to break the Austrian treaty and dissolve the alliance. It's the most disrespectful thing he could have done, and the room is buzzing with gossip.

Peter stands once more, making another announcement. "I have also made the following appointments; I have welcomed back to court, and back to my privy council, Count Lestocq, and the position of chancellor will now be taken by Lord Mikhail Andrei."

More weak applause as Mikhail, seated to the right of Elizavetta, stands and bows at the neck to the assembled guests. By now, George is standing at our table. I feel myself staring at him in stark disbelief, a queasy wave rolling in my stomach.

"Your Majesties," he says, bowing first to Peter, and then to me.

"Uncle George," I finally manage, not meeting his eyes as I scoop up my glass to take a long drink of wine. "How… lovely to see you again. And how unexpected."

Peter turns to me, beaming. I feel the warmth fade from my face, making me shiver.

My mouth instantly parches, and I take another drink to combat the dryness. Peter motions to the empty seat to my left and George bows again, circling the table to sit at my side. I feel myself tense as the steward brings him a plate of food. He still carries the same odor as the day he tried to force himself upon me when I was just a girl, the stale aroma of brandy and cigars. I watch him out of the corner of my eye. My uncle and would-be husband. He'd practically forced the arrangement upon my father, at my mother's insistence, when she believed my chances of courting Peter had failed. His hair is steel gray, his face thin, wrinkled, and pockmarked. Despite his rank of prince, he is a ruffian. It's evidenced by the callous way he speaks, by his yellow fingernails, and his general lack of decorum. He is not a man of political prowess or keen knowledge. So why on earth has Peter chosen him to lead the Russian Army?

Frederick. Of course. Frederick must know he has Peter's favor, but that might not be enough, should the fickle brat king ever turn against Prussia. Fredrick would need someone loyal to him in high rank, positioned perfectly to seize control of Russian forces, should the need arise.

As the feast goes on, I push my food around my plate but eat nothing; rather I listen to Peter and George as they speak around me as if I wasn't even there. I stare at my plate, not looking up or attempting to join in the discussion. Let them forget me. God willing, I might become opaque and fade from the room entirely, leaving only my ears behind that I might know more of their plans.

"And the new guard is in place?" Peter asks, drawing my interest.

George speaks around a mouthful of roast duck, juice dripping from his mouth and into the wiry hair of his beard. "Yes, Your Majesty. The Holstein Cuirassier are here and ready to replace the palace guard."

"Good," Peter says, stabbing another small potato. "I will announce the changing of the guard tomorrow. They will be the bodyguard of the Imperial household. And how much better I will sleep under their protection," he offers with a wink.

I turn. "Peter, I wonder if I might keep my small guard."

He blinks, as if he can't understand why I'd ask for such a thing. "Just my handful of personal guards. I know they are certainly inferior in strength and skill to the new guards, but I simply haven't the energy to learn an entire new set of names. I've already had to replace so many maids that I feel as if I should begin calling them by numbers." I pause, taking a drink. "Besides, I'm sure you'd like me to take some new ladies-in-waiting from the Prussian nobles, now that they are our allies once more."

He waves me off, already bored with the whims of women. "Of course, do as you like."

I nod. "Thank you." Standing, I take my leave. "If you'll excuse me. I am exhausted from all the excitement, and I think I must turn in early." Peter waves me off again and I offer my seat to George, who slides into it without hesitation.

I sweep a glance across the room, connecting first with Sergei, and then with Alexander. With a deep sigh, I leave the banquet with Dashka and head for my rooms. Dismissing Dash to her chamber just down from mine, I turn to Grigori. "I am expecting Lord Mananov and General Salkov. Please show them in when they arrive." He bows and takes up his post outside my door.

Once in my rooms, I slide onto the lounge and take a sip of the vodka that has been left for me. The flavor is crisp and hot, and it settles into my fluttering belly. I can't decide what has me more nervous, seeing my beautiful men and having to confess the truth to them, or the fact that my lecherous uncle is downstairs pouring his venomous words into Peter's ear.

I take another drink.

Chapter

Six

My room smells of heavy rose, thanks to the pale pink bouquets recently added to the crystal vases around my chamber. The odor is pleasant, and I allow myself to be distracted while adjusting one of the arrangements. One of the thorns pricks my finger, a tiny drop of blood forming atop my pale skin. I suckle it, trying to keep the crimson from falling onto my gown. In a moment of contemplation, I hold my hands out, examining them closely. My hands are small, I realize, slender and fragile looking. How odd that God would see fit to put so many fragile things in my care. How many lives would these hands hold? How much power and respect could they command? How many hopes, dreams, and hearts would be mine to nurture or crush in these little hands?

I drop them to my sides, praying they are stronger than they look.

My door opens, and Sergei strides in. Grigori closes the door and Sergei bows deeply before crossing the room in three long steps, drawing me into his arms. I let him hold me, basking in the feeling of him for only a moment before I step back, out of his grasp.

"You asked for me?" Sergei begins. His voice is tight, nervous, as if he expects the worst. Grief washes across me like a cold wave, chilling me into my marrow.

"I did. There is something I must confess to you. While you were away, after Rina died, I..." I hesitate. The next words are forced, unwillingly ripped from my throat. "I took Alexander to my bed. I was so lost and in so much pain. He... I..."

I'm not sure what I expect. Rage, perhaps. Bitterness, at least. Anger at my betrayal. But with no hesitation at all, he steps forward, closing the gap between us, and wraps his arms around me once more, laying a kiss on the top of my head.

"I'm sorry I wasn't there when you needed me," he whispers. "Can you forgive me?"

And just like that, he has absolved me of my guilt and taken it upon his own head.

It's far more than I deserve. Even as I cling to him, I know the blame lies squarely on my own shoulders. The door opens again, and I instinctively pull away.

"Lord Mananov," Grigori announces, closing the door once more, leaving the three of us in uncomfortable silence.

I watch as Alexander's face falls. The sound of his boots on the wooden floor is like a slow, measured heartbeat as he approaches us. He'd been hoping I brought him here to be alone, no doubt. I fight to hold my chin up and not wither under the disappointment in his gaze.

"Thank you both for coming. Please, sit." I motion to the couch in the center of the room, taking my own seat in a high-back chair across from it. They obey, each holding themselves rigid, their shoulders tight, their expressions somber.

Looking at them together like this, I realize that despite their similarities, the dark hair, deep-set eyes, and the golden tone of their skin, they are both vastly different. Alexander is smooth shaven, his lips thin and his nose a narrow slope, Sergei seems rougher, a dark, well-groomed line of hair riding the curve of his jaw, his eyes rounder, more open, his face wider. My men, my loves. The two halves of my whole heart. I force myself to swallow before I speak.

"I apologize for the abruptness of this meeting, as well as for keeping you both at arm's length these past weeks," I begin. "Things have been... strained since Elizabeth's death, and I appreciate you both giving me some much-needed breathing room during the transition."

Sergei nods almost imperceptibly, Alexander presses his lips together. Neither speaks.

I continue. "Things are changing, politically, and some of those changes have me uneasy. My uncle's arrival…" I pause, not knowing exactly what to say. "He is extremely dangerous, to Russia, and potentially, to me." My breath catches in my throat as the memory forms, clear and sharp in my mind. George, storming from my father's study, grabbing me by the arms, forcing his mouth on mine until I was sure my face would be black and blue from the abuse. When he finally drew back, it was only to whisper in my ear, *One day, I will have you*, before storming from my house.

I left for Russia the next day.

Receding from the memory, I look up. Sergei looks angry, his hands balled into fists. Alexander just looks worried, as if he wants to reach out to me.

I exhale sharply. I'm stalling, weaving my way around the truth of this meeting, as if delaying it will make it easier. But I know that's a lie, so I summon what courage I can and delve in. "But that is not really why I've asked you both here. Alexander, you know that Sergei has been my—my lover—for some time." He nods, licking his lips. "And Sergei, you know that recently, I have taken Alexander as my lover as well." He frowns, nodding. My hands begin to shake. I clasp them together in my lap, hoping they won't notice, but as soon as I speak again, I can hear the quake in my voice.

Do it, I command myself. If I'm to cut out all of

our hearts, it's best to do it quickly, a sharp blade to spare the torment of a slow death.

"These past weeks, I've been trying to do something unthinkable. I've been trying to force myself to choose between you. But the thought of losing either of you, it's like carving out my own heart. I want you, I *need* you, both. I am a selfish, awful woman and truthfully, I don't deserve either of you. But I love you both, more deeply than I can express. It's not fair, and it's not right, but it's the truth."

I feel a hot tear slip down my cheek, and I wipe it away quickly. "So I have done the most cowardly thing I can do. I've brought you here, to ask you to choose me. I have nothing to say in my defense, other than I love you, and I understand if you can't bring yourselves to share my heart, but that is all I have to offer you. I know it will not be easy. I know it is much—too much, perhaps—to ask of you. But I'm asking nonetheless. If you love me, if you can find it in your hearts to forgive me, then choose me."

They remain motionless for a few more heartbeats, both frozen in stunned shock at my request. It's Sergei who stands first, rounding the couch and turning his back to me. I watch as he brings his hand to his face and holds it there. I wish, more than anything, that he would look at me, so that I might read his expression. My hands grow icy, my mouth dries. In my chest, the first fractures begin, a sharp, quick pain that I expect to get much, much worse.

Alexander stands, opening his mouth as if to speak, but then snaps it closed. I sit, still shaking from head to toe, fighting to hold my composure. *I will not break down*, I order myself. I will not cry, for fear that my tears will sway them, only to have them hate me for it later.

"To be clear, you are telling us that we must share you or lose you altogether. Is that right?" Alexander rakes his hair back with his fingers, not waiting for me to respond. "You refuse to choose between us, so it is we who must suffer. We who must bend to your wishes."

"There was no other solution I could live with. I didn't plan on falling in love with both of you," I say as calmly as I can manage. "But yes. Somehow, you have stolen equal shares of my heart, and if that is not enough for you, then you must go, for your own sake."

"And are we to have equal shares in your bed as well?" Alexander snaps. "Shall we rotate days? Or perhaps we can adopt a weekly schedule? Or a code? You can wear blue when you want me and green when you want him." He jabs a finger toward Sergei, who remains unmoved. "Or is this a test? The one of us who loves you enough to remain, even under these terms, is the victor? Should we make it so simple for you?"

I rise to my feet. "I know I have hurt you, but you will not speak to me in such a way. I am not your whore, or your mistress. You are mine—do you remember?" I let the words hang between us, invoking a promise he made me which feels like a lifetime ago. "You told me once that you would have me in any way I could give myself to you. Or was that pledge the shallow bargain of a man simply looking to get under my skirts?"

I level a flat gaze at him. "You have both pledged yourselves to me in the past, and you have both understood that I am not free to fully offer myself to anyone. There will always be others with whom you will have to share me. You will share me with my nation, with my husband, and with each other, or you will have no share of me at all. That is all I can offer you. Either it is enough, or it is not."

Alexander looks down, his expression unreadable but his hands held in tight fists. Without a word, he shakes his head once and walks out the door, slamming it behind him. I turn to Sergei, who is still looking away from me.

"You know, I never imagined there would be something you could ask of me that I could not give," he says slowly, turning to face me. His eyes are red, but dry, his tone melancholy. "I can't help but wonder if I'd stayed, if I'd come back for you sooner, if you would have turned to him at all. Perhaps this is entirely my fault. If it is, I see now the swift penance I must pay."

"I don't know," I say honestly. "I think the grief

broke down my walls, but as you said once, first love has a way of staying with you... even when you wish it wouldn't. I'm just so sorry to hurt you like this. It was never what I wanted. But I know I have to be honest with you, with both of you." I cross the room, taking his hands in mine. "All I know is that I can't imagine my life without you in it. Please, please don't hate me. I love you."

He lowers his chin. "But you feel the same about him, don't you?"

There's no accusation in his voice, no anger. That makes it worse, I think. I can only nod.

He takes a deep, shaky breath as he brings my fingers to his lips and lays a gentle kiss across my knuckles. "Who am I to deny the heart of an empress? I'm just a man, flesh and bone, and every single piece of me belongs to you."

Relief floods through me, weakening my knees, and I step forward into his arms. Raising my lips to his, I kiss him, deeply, urgently, with all the ferocity and passion I have been holding so carefully inside myself for so long. His hands curl around my waist, one sliding up to cup the back of my neck. He pulls back just a fraction of an inch, pressing his forehead against mine.

"I chose you. Without doubt, fear, or reason. I will always choose you," he pledges.

With those simple words, he lifts me into his arms and carries me to the bedchamber.

Chapter

SEVEN

I take ill the next morning. Thankfully, Sergei has long past retired to his own chamber when the vomiting begins.

This time there is no doubt in my mind what has happened.

Dashka stays with me, pressing a cool rag to my head as I lie curled on my side on the floor by the sick pan. The cool, parquet floor offers a small measure of relief. Exhaustion wracks my body, but I can't close my eyes or the world tilts and the bile rises up again.

"Should I call for the physician?" she asks for what seems like the hundredth time.

"No, Dash, please. I'm fine."

The truth is… I'm far from fine. I'm with child again. Only this time, there can be no doubt of the paternity. The child can only belong to Alexander, from our encounter weeks past.

One night of love. One night of passion. One night of solace.

How it has wrecked me.

When the spinning room finally stills, I sit up, leaning against Dash for support. She's still in her shift as well. She'd come running when my guard, hearing my distress, had summoned her from her bed to tend to me. She cradles me in her small arms, rocking me gently and singing a soft, sweet tune.

The child is not Peter's. There will be no way to convince him otherwise. He will know the truth of my latest betrayal. If he presses the matter, I could be charged with treason and adultery. The punishment is death.

I take a long, deep breath, blowing it out slowly as I force my mind to focus.

Peter and I have a tenuous peace, at best. I know he would rage at the truth, and I have no doubt he would see me hang for my disloyalty. Then, he could set Elizavetta as his queen, as he's always wanted.

No, Peter cannot know. He can never know.

My mind churns, grasping for solutions.

There are herbs. I remember Mother speaking of them once to the kitchen maid in our old home. There are herbs that can end a pregnancy, if taken soon, before the child is strong enough to resist them.

As soon as the thought comes, I push it away. My hand cups my still-flat belly without thinking about it. I would not harm my child, Alexander's child.

There must be some other way.

Sergei will know. The thought of bringing this news to him, especially now, makes me pitch forward and retch again. It feels as if my heart will climb up and spew out my throat with the rest of my insides. I settle back, Dash wiping at my face gently.

"What can I do?" she begs.

I shake my head. "Nothing now. Nothing but keep my secrets. This one included." I twist my head to look at her. "Can you do that? No one must know. You will have to help me hide it."

She presses her lips together and nods. "Yes, of course. Anything."

"Good, good," I murmur, lying back against her for a bit longer.

By midday, I'm mostly recovered, sitting in my chamber nibbling on some crackers between sips of lavender tea, when my guard opens my door.

"Count Mercy to see you, Your Highness."

I nod and straighten myself in the chair, folding my hands demurely as he enters. Slipping the blue velvet hat from his head, he bows gracefully.

"Your Highness, please pardon the intrusion."

"Not at all, please, have a seat," I offer, motioning to the chair across from me. "What can I do for you today, Count?"

He sits, holding his floppy brim hat in his lap, squeezing it between his fingers. When he speaks, he keeps his eyes downcast, not meeting my glance.

"His Highness has withdrawn all Russian troops

from Berlin. Our armies have had to abandon the city and retreat back to Austria. Empress Maria is quite displeased. News has reached her of Peter's new treaty with Prussia, and she has ordered me back to her side."

The news is nothing I didn't expect. Peter is nothing if not predictable in his love for Prussia—and King Frederick. "I will be sad to see you go. You are a good man, Count Mercy, and I'm saddened that our relationship has been sullied by the change of events."

He sits back, straightening. "I must speak plainly, for my time here is short. Austria and her allies, we have seen things here at court. Even the Russian lords and generals speak of it, of their displeasure at the new regime."

Now it's my turn to sit back, taking a sip of tea to give myself a moment to compose my next words before speaking. "With any change of leadership, there will always be dissenters. There will always be those who preferred the old ways, who are resistant to change. Tides will always change, Count. Fighting against it is futile, and fruitless."

"I think, Your Highness, it is the direction of the tide that worries some. There are rumors…"

I stop him with a gentle laugh. "There are always rumors. If I had a kopek for every rumor swirling around court, I could rebuild the Tower of Babel out of pure gold."

He smiles, but it doesn't quite reach his eyes, "Of course. I only mean to say that, in my time here, and during my visits to Oranienbaum during your residence, I have witnessed what a wise, fair, and just leader you are. You are loved by the gentry and commoners alike. It is my humble observation that His Highness owes the support of his lords and his Russian army directly to you."

I take another sip of tea. "You flatter me."

He pauses before continuing. "I don't mean it as flattery. It is simply a fact. Any man with open eyes can see it. It is your temperance, and your council, that keeps the throne secure."

"One of a wife's greatest duties is keeping her husband's council, offering strength and support when it is needed," I say modestly. "Are you here to ask me to bend his ear toward sustaining our friendship with Austria? Because I fear that ship has sailed."

"No. I think you are quite right on that. I only wish you to know, that should the tides change again, and if you should ever see yourself struggling at the head of them, you have an ally in Austria, and in me."

The blood in my veins freezes, and I have to set my cup down to keep it from spilling into my lap. I blink, reading his expression and finding only sincerity.

In one subtle conversation, Count Mercy has offered me Austrian aid, should I ever choose to usurp the throne of Russia from Peter.

The idea is as laughable as it is terrifying.

I nod and he departs, leaving me to ponder his offer and the choices that have led me to even consider it.

At supper that night, I notice that Count Mercy and Baron de Breteuil have gone from court. Sitting at the head of their usual table is a man I recognize as Baron von Goltz, a Prussian envoy. He'd been at court when I first arrived, when Elizabeth was initially considering a treaty with Frederick. Peter is celebrating his new alliance with his usual boisterous mixture of alcohol and decadence. I sit to his right, Elizavetta to his left. Between dances, he drapes himself on her, laughing drunkenly. As I sweep a gaze across the room, I realize something. There is a division amongst the guests. It's subtle, barely noticeable, but once I see it, it feels blatant, unmistakable.

On the right side of the massive banquet hall most of the lords, the Privy Council, and the head members of the Synod sit. Around the edge of the room, my guards stand, their sharp, green-and-black Russian uniforms tight, swords at each hip. On the other side of the room, a handful of the younger nobles sit, along with a few visiting ladies and a handful of Prussian diplomats, including Von Goltz and his company. The wall on the left is lined with Peter's Holstein guard, their bright blue uniforms tight and uncomfortable looking.

Mikhail sits to my right, an oddity since his normal place is beside Peter. He must see me taking stock because he leans in, whispering. "Just spotted it, have you? It's been this way for a few weeks now, since Peter announced the treaty."

I pull the corners of my mouth into a forced smile, leaning in as I raise a goblet to cover my lips. "Has he noticed yet?"

Mikhail shakes his head. "No, I doubt he would, even if it were pointed out."

"What has Peter been up to these past days?" I finally ask. "He's been unusually quiet."

"Lestocq is back at court. He has Peter hammering out some reforms for the church. And other things."

Count Lestocq, once an ally, had plotted with my own mother to try to free Ivan, Peter's cousin and rival for heir to the throne of Russia, to smuggle him to Prussia and raise an army at his back to depose Elizabeth.

"Why on earth would he have Lestocq return? He knows of the man's part in the conspiracy."

Mikhail nods, staring at Peter, who has taken to the center of the room and is dancing in a salacious manner with not just Elizavetta, but another young lady as well.

"Lestocq has convinced him that they only sought to end Elizabeth's reign because they found her unjust. Peter is prone to believe anything sanctioned by Frederick must be an action worthy of praise, even if that action likely would have ended in his own death."

I shake my head, disappointed but not surprised. "I will speak to him."

"I pray he will listen," he says, raising his glass to me before taking a long drink of wine.

By the time I retire for the evening, Peter is nearly unable to stand. I watch as he's half carried off to his chamber by Alexander, who doesn't even spare me a glance as he passes by. Elizavetta, staggering but somehow still on her feet, follows, wine bottle firmly in hand.

I don't sleep that night. Lying in bed, I rub my belly absently, trying to imagine a life where I could have my child, where I could live in peace, without always looking over my shoulder for enemies or having to manipulate those around me. Silly, really, that when I look around at my chamber, at the fresh roses, the silk tapestries, and the ornate gold filigree etched into every wall from parquet floor to vaulted ceiling, I would find myself longing for a simple life, for a cottage and a clutch of chickens and a husband who holds my hand next to a simple stone hearth at night.

Perhaps we only long for things we cannot possess.

When morning comes, the sickness returns and is slowly calmed with ginger tea and biscuits. As soon as I dress, I make my way to Peter's chamber, followed by a maid holding a tray of coffee and fresh bread. He will be feeling the full effects of last night, and I will have a better chance of swaying him if he's being coddled.

His page moves to announce me, but I wave him off. "Best not go in yelling," I gently say, pressing the double doors open and stepping inside.

The door to the far chamber is open. After motioning for the maid to leave the tray, I pour a cup of coffee and head to the back. Elizavetta is naked, her curvy, freckled body only half obscured in the tangle of blankets. Peter is upside down in the bed, still fully dressed from last evening. Reaching down, I touch his shoulder.

"Peter?"

He mutters, throwing an arm across his face. "Go away."

I gently shake him. "Peter, it's morning. I've brought you some coffee."

"Blast it, woman, let me rest."

I step back, tapping the side of the cup with my fingernail, making a clicking noise. Finally, he rolls his head to the side, glaring at me through one half-opened eye. I hold up the cup. "There's whiskey in it."

He sighs heavily and rolls off the bed, stumbling before managing to upright himself.

"Why are you here so early?" he demands, snatching the cup from my hand and walking limply past me. Once he's in the outer chamber, I pull his bedroom door closed, letting his mistress remain in her deep, noisy slumber.

"It's after midday, Peter, truly. You have to meet with the Synod in an hour. I wanted to make sure you were woken gently. But next time, I will be happy to leave you to your grooms, if you prefer."

He frowns. Of all the people in the palace, his grooms, both elderly men with little patience, were the least likely to pity his current condition, and we both know it.

I take a seat as he paces, sipping the coffee with disinterest.

"So, what is your meeting today about?" I ask as if absently. "Are you instituting some pro-Protestant reform?"

He snickers. "Something like that."

That piques my curiosity. "Are you going to tease me, or may I know of your dastardly plans?" I keep my tone light, joking.

"Well, if you must know, I'm ordering all the idols and saints be removed from places of worship. And I'm also demanding each church give half of their collected tithe to the crown." He pauses, taking another drink as he looks past me, out the window overlooking the gardens. "And I think I will have them shave their beards, as a display of fealty to their new king."

I wait, hoping he'll turn and smile, and it will all be some terrible jest. But when he looks at me, he's stone faced and deadly serious. I open my mouth just a little, saying nothing but running my tongue along my teeth. Do I dare stand against him in this? My own situation is precarious; to point out that his move may lose him even more loyalty would be a mistake. Especially since that loyalty seems to be swinging in my direction. Should he ever take notice, should he ever perceive me as a potential threat, his retribution will be swift and merciless.

"Do you have an opinion on the matter?" he asks, his voice a clear challenge.

I look down. "I fear for you, husband. I fear that by bringing Lestocq back to court, that he might not have your best interests at heart."

"Lestocq? He is my man, trustworthy in every way."

"He would have usurped the throne for Ivan," I blurt out, unable to stop myself. "They would have put him on the throne in your place, and possibly worse."

"If you think that Fredrick would have harmed me, you are gravely mistaken. He loves me as his own son."

"Fredrick loves only himself and his nation. He would rule Russia, and he would use your love to do it." I hear my voice rising, but I can't seem to bring myself to heel. "I love Prussia as well as you; it was my home also, once. But we are Russia now. Our priorities must lie with her. You must carefully consider your actions. There is a fine line between being an ally to Prussia and being a puppet to King Frederick."

He hastily tosses the cup onto the table, cracking it. "And you think me a puppet? A simpleton with no mind of his own?"

I take a step back. "I think your love for Fredrick, your trust in him, blinds you to his true ambition. And Lestocq is a servant of that ambition, make no mistake."

He waves me off. "He has given me reason enough to trust him. Come see."

He sweeps past me, throwing open his chamber doors and leading me down the corridor. We weave through the maze of halls until we arrive at a small chamber near the counsel room. He pushes the door open and, taking me by the arm, pulls me inside.

The chamber is meager, but comfortable. A small, four-poster bed draped in a damask canopy is at the center. When Peter arrives, a slender, hunched boy throws back the blankets and rushes to his side, falling to one knee. His hair is long and un-groomed, but he's clean and in a fresh linen shift. When he looks up at me, something tugs at the center of my mind, a familiarity which I cannot seem to place.

Then I see it, the family resemblance. The boy looks so much like his grandfather, whose painting hangs in the grand hall, that it's uncanny. I feel my hand fly to my chest of its own will. "Ivan?"

The boy furiously shakes his head, lowering his chin further into his chest and muttering.

I turn to Peter, who is smiling like a fox. "You see, little mother? I handed Ivan to Lestocq myself. He turned me down flat. They have no interest in him. His mind is addled from his imprisonment." He lowers his voice. "He doesn't even know who he is. Isn't that funny? I call him Pigeon."

Peter pats the boy's head and laughs.

Stepping forward I slap his hand away. "Are you mad? You can't bring him here and keep him like some pet! He is the heir of Empress Anna and a legitimate rival for your throne."

"Frederick will not have him; he would not even try to use him against me."

"If not Fredrick, than it will be some other. You have well managed to make enemies of France and Austria. What if word of his presence spreads? Either of them could fund an uprising against you with him as the figurehead," I practically scream in his face, finally at my limits with his idiocy. I motion to the boy, who scurries around the bed, hiding behind the headboard. "This, this is political castration, Peter. Surely, you can see that?"

I don't see the blow coming, so when it lands, an open-handed slap to my face, it rocks me from my feet and I sprawl to the floor.

"Don't think to challenge my wisdom, Catherine." He spits my name like bitter milk. "No one will challenge me because they love me. They adore me. You saw them, each pledging fealty to me as I rode into St. Petersburg. Even Count Mercy begged me to let him remain. You would poison me against Frederick, but his heart is the same as mine, and it beats for Prussia!"

I struggle to my feet, my face still stinging from the blow, my lips quickly swelling. Curling my fingers into a tight fist, I step forward and swing, landing my blow to his jaw with an impact that seems to instantly shatter all the bones in my hand. Peter falls back, his head smacking against the floor with a dull thud. He looks up at me, disoriented.

Leaning over him, I speak. "You will never raise a finger to me again or I swear to holy God that I will geld you in your sleep. You will return Ivan to wherever you found him, and you will do it immediately. He isn't just a threat to you, but to me and our child as well. Let go of your foolish grasp on Prussia, Peter. It will be the death of you."

"You hit me," he whispers, in disbelief, clutching the side of his face. "You can't hit me. I'll have you flogged for this!"

"Oh? Then call the guard. I'm sure your soldiers will get a good laugh when they hear about how your wife laid you flat on your ass with one swing!" My chest heaves with rage as I shout. Finally, uncurling my hand with a wince of pain I try very hard to conceal, I straighten.

"Is that a threat?" he demands as I turn to leave, my skirts swishing behind me. "You can't threaten me!"

I turn back to him, slowly, keeping my expression neutral. "Everything I do, I do to protect you, to protect our son, and to protect Russia. I am not your enemy, Peter. Please don't force me to be one."

As soon as I'm out the door, I press my back against the wall, stuff my aching fist in my mouth, and scream.

Chapter

EIGHT

When Sergei arrives in my chamber, I'm soaking my red knuckles in a bowl of cool water and salts.

"What happened?" he asks, pressing himself along my back, cradling me with one arm while examining my fingers with the other.

"It's Peter. I struck him," I admit, unable to keep the exhaustion from my voice. He leans forward, pressing his face into my neck and leaving a gentle kiss on my collar.

"You struck him?" His tone is a mixture of pride and exasperation. "Catherine, what were you thinking? He could have you flogged for such a thing."

I turn in his arms, our faces nearly touching. "He's brought Ivan here, to the palace."

"Ivan? Why on earth would he do that?"

I pull away so I can pace as I let the entire story tumble from my lips. He listens, his expression never wavering.

"I will retrieve the boy, take him back to the prison," he flatly says. "I'll go now, before anyone discovers he was ever here."

I shake my head. "He can't go back there. He must be taken somewhere Peter can never find him again. You didn't see him, Sergei. He's more animal than man, too many years of darkness and abuse. I don't want to see him live out his days in such a manner, but he can't stay here like Peter's personal dog either."

Sergei is quiet for a minute, considering. "There's a small village near Peterhoff. I can take him there; give him into the custody of the church as a nameless beggar. Do you think he is sound enough to dispute it?"

"No, I think not. Peter calls him Pigeon. I doubt he even knows his real name anymore."

Slowly, hesitantly, Sergei takes my hand. "There is another way to be sure no one can use the boy against you. Perhaps it would be even more merciful."

A shiver rips through me at his words, spoken so gently, but holding such deadly promise.

"No, I would not have him killed if I can help it," I say firmly. "But be sure the monks know that should anyone ever come for him, should any attempt be made to take him from their care..." I let that sit between us, my edict unspoken but unmistakable. If anyone should try to remove him from their care, he must be killed immediately. "Be certain to offer them enough coin to ensure their silence—and their loyalty."

"They will do as their empress commands." Sergei nods, his expression as unwavering as ever. "But please, be more cautious with treating Peter. I know how difficult he can be, but you mustn't turn his temper in your direction."

I smile at his gentle chastisement. "I know, my love, truly. Still, I can't put into words just how wonderful it felt, in the moment."

He laughs. "I hope someday to discover it for myself."

With that, he kisses me tenderly and takes his leave.

Later, I watch nervously as he leads the boy from his room and into a waiting carriage. The poor, broken boy swings his eyes my way only once, his expression sorrowful and confused. Part of me demands to protect him, to try to heal the terrible damages that have been done to him, but the other part wants only to be free of the threat that his still-beating heart represents.

The following week, Peter signs his new declaration into law, against the advisement of his privy council and the Synod. That day, I receive two letters and a private audience with the most influential cardinals in Russia. Each of them begs me to intercede on their behalf, but I cannot. When the Archbishop of Novgorod arrives, seeking an audience, I know too well what he wants. After a few moments of exchanging pleasantries, he gets to the matter at hand.

"His Highness came to me yesterday seeking a divorce," he flatly states. I feel my mouth gape open. The archbishop looks different than I remember, younger perhaps, with his freshly shaven cheeks, but there is a sadness in his features now that once remained hidden. "He says that if we do not grant him this measure, that he will secularize all church property and ban any outdoor services, and I have no doubt of his sincerity on the matter. He has already ordered clergy to wear black cassocks like Protestant pastors. We've been forced to shave our beards; those who refused were tortured or imprisoned. Our once-devoted flocks are now riotous. "

I can only shake my head. "On what grounds does he seek to divorce?" My voice is a whisper, but I know I have brought this upon myself. He has never taken authority well, less so by those he considers beneath him. I pushed him, and now, as Sergei feared, I will pay for it.

"He accused you of everything from adultery to witchcraft. But I want to assure you, I will not allow such wild accusations to spread. I doubt any clergy would support his request, especially now. Many of us have approached the situation with great humility and in fervent prayer, and we believe God will soon strike down those unworthy of their mantles, preserving his faithful. Let not your mind or heart be troubled, Your Highness."

Relief creeps into my skin, numbing me. "So you don't plan to allow the divorce?"

He shakes his head. "No, I will delay for as long as I'm able, and with the last breath in my body."

He stares at me expectantly, as if searching my very soul. It makes me uncomfortable, so I offer him a grateful smile. "Thank you, Your Eminence."

He nods, pulling a worn leather bible from the pocket of his robes. "Will you spare a moment to pray with me?"

"Of course."

We kneel together and he offers a solemn prayer, but I can't bring myself to focus on his words.

Peter has finally done it, what he's always threatened to do. He's decided to cast me aside, divorce me and make Elizavetta his wife. Perhaps it's not as soon as she hoped, but her ambition for the crown seems to have no end. She will keep pushing him now; continue building the wall between us until we are so far apart that nothing could bring us together again. And worst of all, I laid the foundation for it myself.

As it stands, he lacks the leverage to force the divorce, legally, but if he discovers the child...

When the archbishop takes his leave, I'm left alone in my chamber, my hands on my still-flat stomach, praying for guidance I'm certain I don't deserve.

Peter soon discovers the boy missing and storms into my chamber where Dashka and I sit, sewing, while we wait for supper.

"What have you done?" he demands, throwing open the door to my chamber.

I motion for Dash to leave us, which she does without hesitation, slipping out the door and closing it behind her with a soft click.

"I'm afraid you'll need to be more specific," I say absently, not looking up from my stitch until Peter grabs the round table in the corner of the room and flips it, sending a vase of flowers shattering to the ground.

"Ivan. Where is he? Where have you taken my Pigeon?"

I sit calmly, folding my hands in my lap as I set down my needlepoint. "Why on earth would you think I have him?" I ask simply.

He steps forward, looking like he might throttle me. I'm not sure what stops him, but I think I see a flicker of fear pass behind his ice-blue eyes. He points at me. "If I find out you have him, so help me, I will have you thrown in a cell."

I sigh. "I do not have him, Peter. Perhaps he simply wandered off. In his fragile state, he may be prone to sleepwalking or simply getting confused and scared. As I told you, he's not a pet. He's a person."

"*He was mine!*" Peter rages, spittle flying from his mouth. "You did this. You have handed him to my enemies, hoping they will overthrow me."

It's all I can do not to snicker at the assumption. Instead, I pour myself a cup of tea. "Peter, listen to yourself. You've become too paranoid. What good would it do me to see you deposed and Ivan on the throne? They'd likely kill us both, and our son."

"You could be planning to kill me and marry him to keep your status."

I raise my cup, inhaling the aroma deeply before responding. "Peter, the only person looking to end our marriage is you. Perhaps it is your own guilty conscious that plagues you."

He falters, stepping backward.

I raise one eyebrow. "I know you care for Elizavetta, but divorce? Did you really imagine the church would allow it?"

"They will do as they are told."

I take a sip of tea. "Oh, I doubt that. Luckily for me, they obey the mandates of God, not bratty kings tired of their wives."

"I will be free of you, so help me," he stammers.

"Peter, please. We don't have to be at odds. You

have my loyalty, my support. Isn't that enough to earn peace between us, at least?"

He lowers his chin. "If you are truly loyal to me, then you will obey me. I am granting Elizavetta the Order of Saint Catherine. You will award her the ribbon in a ceremony during your birthday celebration next week."

Now it is I who stutters. "But that is an honor reserved for the grand duchess and Romanov Princesses."

He shakes his head, a menacing smile spreading across his face. "The emperor may award it to whomever he sees fit. It's an honor given to any noblewoman worthy of recognition. Her familial ties alone make her worthy; my love makes her more so. You will do this. Is that clear?"

I stiffen, but I grudgingly nod. What can I do? It's an insult, a public display not only of his affection for Elizavetta, but of his disregard for me. A very public, political slap in the face.

I bruised his ego when I struck him. This is simply him striking back, and I should have expected it.

"Of course, Your Majesty."

Satisfied, he turns on his heel and saunters from the room. I close my eyes, taking a slow, deep breath to calm myself. Rage would be wasted, and I haven't the energy for it anyway. This new child is sapping my strength as it grows. Already weary, I'm left to contemplate my next move.

Chapter
NINE

Sergei returns the next morning, and I decide to let him rest from his journey before seeking his counsel on my latest complication.

The child.

As I nibble my dry bread with the afternoon tea, I contemplate telling Alexander. As the father, it is his right to know. But he hasn't so much as glanced at me since our last talk, and part of me simply can't bear to face him now. If he's chosen to leave, I can't let this child bind him to me. It's not fair to any of us.

No, it will have to be kept secret, from everyone except Sergei and of course Dash, who has already sworn herself to silence.

I decide to take a ride that day, while I'm still able, and order the grooms to prepare my horse Peony. Grigori accompanies me, along with Dash, on a slow trek through the woods late that afternoon.

It feels good to be on horseback again, the breeze in my hair, the powerful hooves thundering below me. I go slow, not wanting to risk a fall, but even that is difficult. Part of me wants to loosen the reins and fly through the dense woods. Keeping calm, still, is an effort all its own. Soon, another set of hooves approaches. Grigori draws his sword, bringing his steed to a stop between Dash, me, and the approaching horseman. When I see Sergei's visage break through the trees, I sag with relief. He nods to Grigori, who re-sheaths his sword and lets him pass. Sergei strides up beside me and we trot slowly ahead, leaving Dashka and Grigori a few paces behind.

"Is it done?" I ask.

He nods. "It is done. Ivan is safe; his life there will be more comfortable than a cell at any rate. But, should anyone come for him... the monks will do as you've ordered."

My hands tighten on the reins. "There's something else I need your assistance with," I begin. There's a long pause before I continue, hesitating at admitting the truth, which I know will inflict yet another wound in his heart.

"What is it?" he asks, unable to stand the silence any longer.

Chewing my lip, I force myself to answer. "It's only that I seem to keep hurting you. I never wanted to hurt you. I never wanted things to be this way."

He looks away, facing forward. Probably not wanting to meet my eyes, afraid of what my next blow will be.

"I'm with child again," I finally say.

He pulls his horse to a stop, turning to look at me. For a moment, there's a look of radiant joy in his eyes. At seeing my own sour expression, his face falls. As I watch, the realization of the truth hits him like a blow to the stomach. He leans forward, reaching out to stroke the mare's mane.

"Alexander's?" His tone is light, but sad, and it crushes something inside me.

"Yes." I force the word past my lips.

Taking a deep breath, he seems to right himself. "Does he know?"

I frown. "No. I do not know if he ever will."

Sergei turns to me once more, his bushy eyebrows drawing together. "You must tell him. A father should know."

My heart swells as I stare at his rugged face. My love, my sturdy foundation. There is no bitterness in him; perhaps he's incapable of such darkness. I smile, unable to contain my emotions. "You are the best man I've ever known, Sergei, my love. A lesser man would rage with jealousy. I know I could not bear it if our situations were reversed. How is it possible that your heart can be so strong?"

He grins wickedly. "My queen, a lesser man would crumble under the weight of your love. If I want to keep you, I have no choice but to be strong— and also very flexible. If that is the price of a place in your heart, I will gladly pay it. That, I think, is what

Alexander has yet to understand."

I feel my smile falter. "Perhaps. But if he has chosen to leave me, I would not use this child as a chain to bind him to me."

Scooting closer, Sergei reaches out, placing a hand on mine. "You can't use your anger as an excuse to keep this from him. He is hurting. We are all hurting. Give him time. He's young and only beginning to understand what it is to be loved by a queen."

Though there is no accusation in his voice, I feel it in each word. We are all hurting, and it is my fault. I pull away, my horse skittering to the side. "This is not something I can think of right now. I can't worry for his feelings. I can only do what must be done, for I am no queen yet."

"You are my queen," Sergei declares as we begin moving forward again.

There is only a moment of silence between us before I speak again. "Peter has asked the archbishop to grant him a divorce."

There's a light gasp behind me, meaning Dash has been listening in. I ignore it. Truthfully, it will soon be the worst-kept secret at court. I have no doubt Peter will be singing it in a chorus to anyone who will listen.

I continue forward, looking ahead to the grassy meadow stretching before us. "The church has refused him, for now. There are no grounds, you see.

But if this pregnancy becomes public, if Peter ever finds out... He won't have to divorce me. He can have me executed for adultery."

Beside me, Sergei is quiet, pensive. Sliding my gaze to him, I see that he is struggling with what to say next.

"I considered ending the pregnancy," I admit. "But I simply can't bring myself to do it. My child..." I don't finish the thought. The softening of his expression tells me there is no need to.

"So what is your plan? Shall we take a trip, Moscow perhaps, until the birth?"

"I can't leave Peter here alone right now. He's too erratic. And while he's angry at me, at least I can use my influence with the nobles to try to temper him." I loosen my grip on the reins to find that the leather straps have dug into my skin, chaffing my palms despite my riding gloves.

"You must be so very careful," he finally says. "Any misstep, any hint of the truth, could condemn you."

It's a terrible risk, he's right on that account, but my options are extraordinarily limited. "I know."

The days pass quickly as preparations for my birthday celebration are made. Envoys from all over Europe arrive, gifts in tow, to greet the new empress.

The worst of my morning sickness seemingly over, I take the opportunity to meet every single person and their entourages. Peter spends his time in meetings with his Prussian advisors, Prince George included. He has requested an audience only once, which I refused as politely as possible, feigning exhaustion.

The day begins far too early as Jean rolls my hair into perfect curls, teasing them atop my head. A gown, specially made for the event, is brought in. It's not as cumbersome or as heavy as my wedding gown, but it's very close. Dash helps me dress, taking my corset as small as she dares in my condition, and drapes my red sash across my chest. I frown as I touch the crimson fabric, my fingers running over the silver embroidery which reads, из любви к отечеству.—*for the love of the fatherland.* The day Empress Elizabeth adorned me with it had felt like a victory. Now, knowing I will have to do the same for his mistress, it feels more like a mockery. The latest in a long line of small torments I'm forced to endure. My hands clench, and the ribbon crumples under my fingers.

By the time the herald announces my arrival, I'm weary to my very bones. Weary from the weight of my gown, weary from the timid smile that I must keep etched upon my face, and weary from the heavy choices that haunt my very soul. I stand atop the grand staircase, feeling less like a queen and more like a prisoner who must carefully embrace her own shackles.

"Her Highness, The Empress Catherine."

I glide down the stairs, Dashka at my side, Sergei and Grigori trailing behind, a handful of ladies-in-waiting and dutiful lords following them. Making my way through the assembly, pausing to receive well wishes and kisses on the hand from some of those attending, I make my way toward Peter, who sits atop the highest table. Beside him, in my seat, Elizavetta seers at me a she stabs a bit of duck with a golden fork. To his other side, Prince George looks down at me, his expression nearly apologetic. All the chairs at the head table are occupied, leaving no room for me.

Peter stands, raising his glass. "Let us salute the lovely Catherine on this, the anniversary of her birth."

His informality makes me bristle, but I manage to hold the smile on my face as I bow from the neck at his words. It's meant as a slap in the face, the forgetting of my title, and I am quite done being slapped by my idiot husband.

The assembly claps riotously and when the noise dies down, I shoot a glare at Peter. "Would Your Highness allow me the privilege of dining among his loyal lords this evening?" I ask, my voice clear. I watch as a tick forms in his jaw. He was hoping to use my displacement as yet another show of his disapproval of me, but now, with my asking, I have made it seem as if it were my choice. Finally, he nods, waving his hand as if unimpressed before retaking his seat and turning to whisper something into Elizavetta's ear.

I turn to the crowd, a wide smile on my face. "Which of you would be so kind as to offer your empress a seat at your table so that I might know you better?" I jovially ask. Immediately, a half a dozen men stand, bowing.

I glide down the hall, continuing to greet and chat with the attending nobles before finally settling on a seat at the table with Lord Ashburn and his wife, one of my ladies-in-waiting, Lady Janiette. Lord Ashburn flushes, his rugged face practically glowing with pride as I take a seat beside him. He is one of the wealthiest and most influential of the lords, and he holds title to most of the lands to the north of Moscow. He also has a vast personal army and, rumor says, a heartfelt distaste for his new sovereign's alliance with Prussia. I spend the evening making small talk, and then, finally, dancing the hours away.

Though I am tired, dreadfully so, I keep the façade going until Peter finally interrupts the gathering late in the evening. When he stands, the musicians stopping mid-song, his words are slurred and his face blotchy from too much wine.

"It seems only fitting that the final gift of the evening be presented by Catherine herself." He pauses to belch, and then motions for Elizavetta to stand.

She smiles, gathering her massive blue gown, obviously designed to complement the blue Prussian uniform jacket Peter now wears, and makes her way to the floor.

As gracefully as possible, I thank my latest dance partner and wave to Dash, making my way toward Elizavetta. Her green eyes shine. Her grin is wide and sour.

"This evening, by command of his Imperial Highness, I have been asked to present the Ribbon of The Order of Saint Catherine to Lady Elizavetta Vorontsova for her..." I pause, clearing my throat suggestively, "*exhaustive* dedication to crown and country." A snicker rolls through the crowd. Dash steps forward, holding out the box that contains a sash identical to mine. I drape it over Elizavetta, carefully moving her long, ginger ringlets off her shoulder.

I step back, turning away from her and toward the assembly. They unenthusiastically clap. A murmur cuts through the room like a swift undercurrent. If anyone was unaware of Peter's intention to divorce me, there is no doubt now.

I wave my hand, and the music begins again. Sergei steps forward, bowing formally and holding up a hand in a request to dance. I take it, grateful for him, for his strength, and for his ability to anticipate my needs in ways I never seem able to. It's his borrowed courage that keeps me on my feet, long after the music has stopped.

Chapter

TEN

The next day, Prince George requests an audience. Though I want desperately to refuse him, I know I cannot afford the luxury of denial. He, as one of few who have Peter's ear, could have valuable information. I send for tea and greet him with what I hope is a tolerant, if not friendly, smile.

He takes both my hands in his and leans forward to press a kiss on my cheek. "Your Highness," he begins. "My lovely niece, how you have grown."

His words hold no malice, yet they send a chill into my neck. "Uncle George. It is lovely to see you as well."

I sit, motioning him to a chair across the table from me. "Please. Have a seat. What it is that I can do for you today?"

He snickers. "Straight to business, I see."

I take a cup of tea from the maid, raising one eyebrow. "Unfortunately, ruling a country leaves little time for wasting on insignificant chatter," I say as gently as possible. "And to be honest, I find I haven't the stomach for it. Especially when my husband is threatening to divorce me. You wouldn't know anything about that, would you?"

I do not try to conceal the accusation in my tone. The smile falls from his face, replaced by a frown. "I assure you, I had no idea."

His false modesty raises my hackles. I set my tea on the silver tray with a clatter. "Then I doubt there is anything you might say that would be of interest to me. If that is all?"

He takes a deep breath, looking sufficiently chastised. "No, I mean, yes. I mean, I only meant that I had no part in his decision."

I sit back, resting my hands in my lap. "What have you come to tell me?"

He strokes his chin absently before speaking. "You are more beautiful than I remember, but you are not the same innocent, naive little girl I once knew."

"No, I am not. I am your empress and I think you should keep that firmly in mind when you choose your next words," I openly threaten.

"Of course." He bows his head meekly. "I wanted to come and tell you that, whatever you may think of me, I am not your enemy. Actually, I should quite like to be your ally."

Sitting forward I reach for my tea once more and take a dainty sip. "Pretty words, Prince George. But your actions seem less genuine."

"I know you think I'm here as a spy for King Fredrick, but I assure you, that is the least of my motivations. The simple truth is that Peter is unpredictable. His love for Prussia is strong now, but once he fully realizes his own power, even that devotion may fall into jeopardy. This is something Fredrick is well aware of."

"Then why didn't you seize Ivan when you had the chance? I know Peter offered him to you."

"Ivan, I'm sure you saw with your own eyes, is too badly broken to be useful, even as a headpiece. The country would never rally to him. Not in the way they would rally to you."

And there it is. He has set the bait, a trap meant to lure me into treachery against my husband, giving him all he needs to have me arrested and beheaded.

"If you have come here to try to persuade me to rise against my husband, your efforts are wasted. I will not challenge him. His is the rightful and sovereign ruler of Russia."

He holds up his hand. "Of course. I would not ask you to speak or act against His Highness. I only wish to point out one thing."

"And what is that?"

"His Highness is emperor in title only. He has yet to be properly crowned and anointed. Baron von Goltz has been begging Peter daily to perform the necessary ordinances, but Peter refuses. He claims there is no need for archaic ceremonies, and that he is the true and undisputed ruler."

I sit back, surprised by the news. I had assumed Peter was simply waiting until he was rid of me so he could be crowned beside his wife of choice.

When I say nothing, George continues. "You must see how dangerously vulnerable this makes him appear to foreign powers. A king who refuses to assume the rightful mantle? It invites talk of un-suitability."

I nod.

"And should you ever find yourself in need of an ally, please know you can count on me."

I stare at him, carefully weighing his words. What do I know about my dear uncle? I know he is shrewd and has little tolerance for people he deems below him. I know he will take what he wants, if given the chance, but that his word is sacred to him as it once was to my father. They come from a breed of men who value honestly above all else. Still, I cannot bring myself to trust him.

"Your council, and your offer, are appreciated," I say as I stand. Taking his cue to exit, he bows deep-ly and leaves my chamber. Turning to my maid, I hand her my now-empty teacup. "Please have the valet summon Lord Salkov. I would speak with him urgently."

She curtsies and hurries off to do my bidding. Before she can reach the door, it flies open, nearly knocking her to the ground. Grigori stands in the archway, his face stern.

"Your Highness, your son has been taken."

An hour later, I'm pacing in the throne room. We normally only use this area for greeting visitors and holding open court, but now there is an ominous tone to its empty stillness. Grigori stands at the door, speaking in hushed tones with the house guards. Peter's golden throne, sitting in front of the massive imperial crest on red tapestry, is empty. Even news that our son has been taken from his nurses during a day trip to the village isn't enough to pry him from his childish games. I turn my focus once more to the wooden floor beneath my feet as I walk the black inlaid lines in pattern. Finally, a door to the rear left of the throne opens and Peter saunters in, George at one side and Mikhail at the other.

One of the house guards rushes forward, dropping quickly to one knee as Peter flops into his throne.

"Your Highness, my men are searching the village house by house. Guards have been sent to every road in and out, and we are questioning witnesses as we speak."

Peter waves his hand. "The boy probably simply wandered off. I'm sure we will find him soon enough."

I'm so shocked by his careless tone that it takes my breath for a moment. I close the distance between us in three long, rage-filled strides. "How can you possibly say that? He is surrounded by nurses and guards at all times! There is no way he could have simply wandered off. He was obviously taken, and considering that he is your only heir, I'd think you'd give this threat the swift and severe retribution it warrants." I'm practically shouting, but I can't seem to stop myself. His gaze swings to me.

"Who would have taken him? No one would dare. My people love me."

"And what of the enemies you've made of Austria and France? Perhaps it was their agents who have stolen our son," I say, my hysteria growing. "If he dies, your entire reign is in jeopardy. Do you not realize that? Without a legitimate heir to succeed you, you become an easy target for anyone who would seek to unsettle Russia."

I level a glare at George, who upon seeing my unspoken question, shakes his head. Fredrick had nothing to do with this, he tells me without words.

Mikhail speaks. "She is right, Your Highness. We must treat the matter as a political threat until we have proof otherwise."

Peter mumbles something. George and Mikhail gather close to him, blocking my view. Spinning on my heel, I stride to Grigori. "Is there any news?" I beg.

He bows, his fist on his heart. "I believe we may have a witness. I would like to send my own men to question the man."

"Of course. *Go*. Go yourself if you think you can bring my son back to me."

He bows again. "Yes, Your Highness. I will return with your son or not at all."

Once he's gone, I turn back to Peter. He's sitting on the throne, leaning haphazardly over one side, laughing at something he's just said. Inside me, rage builds like an ember being fanned to flame. There have been many abuses I've tolerated, many hurts I've tried to brush off. But this is something I will never forgive and never forget. In my silent rage, I find a thread of strength and I cling to it the way the sky clings to the last dying rays of sunlight.

It's then that I realize something.

Pain changes you. You can choose to release it and let it leave its scars, or you can wind it up inside yourself and let it become your weapon.

And in that moment, I make my choice.

I pace the floor until nightfall, letting the rage bubble in my mind. Peter is long gone and I am alone, save for Dash, who sits in a single chair by the window, watching the stars appear in the sky. When Sergei strides in, I rush to him without hesitation and he takes me into his arms.

"Is there any news?" I ask, clutching his emerald-green jacket like a small child.

He kisses my forehead, sending reassuring warmth through my tense body. "No, but the house guard is leaving no stone unturned."

I sigh, my shoulders falling forward as I step back and turn away from him, resuming my pacing. Before I can step away, he takes me by the arm, gently turning me back to him. When he speaks, his gaze is stern, his voice low. "I am as concerned as you. I've been searching myself all day. I'm only back for supplies and to see how you are doing."

I nod. "I'm as well as you can expect. Peter seems to think it's all some jest or that he simply wandered off. It's as if he doesn't care at all that his heir is missing."

"Shall I stay?" he asks, taking my hand. "I can fetch some wine and biscuits and we can sit here, together."

I shake my head. "No, as much as I would relish your company, I think I'd feel better knowing you were searching as well."

"Of course," he consoles. "Please, let Dash see you to your chambers so you can try to rest. I will send word as soon as I find him. And don't lose hope. I'm confident we will return him to your arms."

I reluctantly agree, earning me a chaste kiss before he turns to leave. Once he's gone, Dash is at my side.

"Come, Your Majesty. Let's get you to bed." She holds her hand out and I accept the gesture, letting her lead me to my chamber as if in a daze.

After the gown, jewels, and crown are stripped away, I stand, cold beneath my nightdress, and stare at my bed. "Dash, will you stay with me?" I ask, not wanting to face the silence of the night.

"Of course," she meekly says. "I'll go change and be right back."

I crawl into bed, certain my eyes will never close, and wait for her to change and return. She slides into bed beside me, and we snuggle in. The low, rhythmic sound of her breath lulls me into a restless slumber.

I'm awake before dawn breaks, which means I've slept four hours at most, but as soon as my eyes open, my mind spins. What if something terrible has happened to Paul? How afraid he must be, so far from home and the people he knows. I wonder if he cries for me, or for the nurses he knows far better. I've been negligent with him, not visiting as often as I should, certainly seeing him less than Rina and I had seen her son. In that moment, I close my eyes, praying for his safety, for the chance to set it right, for the opportunity to hold him once more. Dash calls for an early breakfast, and we are dressed and back in the throne room before most of the palace even wakes.

The Archbishop of Novgorod sweeps into the room, his robes fluttering in the breeze as he walks. We pray together for some time before a commotion jars me from my reverence.

There's a bustle outside in the corridor, voices raised as trumpets sound.

Finally, the doors blow open and Grigori rushes in, my little boy clinging to him, unconscious. I rush to them, holding out my arms. Is Paul hurt? Dead? My heart pounds furiously. Then I see the slow, rhythmic rise and fall of his small chest. Asleep. Probably exhausted from the ordeal.

Grigori releases Paul into my arms, and the small child stretches from his slumber. I stare down at his face, more a boy now and less a babe, and for one horrifying, bone-chilling moment, I see Peter's face reflected back at me. I collapse to the ground, still cradling him against my bosom. His head rolls onto my shoulder and he blinks, his glacier-blue eyes staring up at me.

The tears come with no warning, with no fanfare. Hot and salty, they spill down my cheeks and onto my lips. I'd been so sure he wasn't Peter's son that I had convinced myself. Perhaps that's why I'd stayed away. I told myself I had simply been too busy to visit him, but perhaps deep down, part of me knew the truth all along. I denied it to myself, but now I see it with stunning clarity. And some small, broken part of me that I cannot forgive myself for is disgusted by it. I cry because I wish I didn't feel this way, because I want to be a better mother than my own was to me, and because I still can't forgive the circumstances in which he was conceived.

This, my child, is yet another part of my life poisoned by Peter and his cruelty.

By the time Peter strides in, Grigori has already explained what he discovered in the town by the river where they finally found my son—not that I absorb any of the news. Only now am I beginning to calm enough to take full stock of his words. I listen numbly, cradling my child in both relief and grief, as he retells the saga to Peter.

"The men who stole him are in the courtyard, tied to the block. They say they were acting on no one's orders, though at least one of them is Dutch. We did find a ledger that leads us to believe the men are smugglers, probably looking to hold His Highness for ransom to the crown. We will interrogate them further," Grigori offers with a bow.

"No," Peter interjects. "I will question them myself."

Looking up through my tears, I see a look of anticipation etched into his features. I remember all too well how Peter likes to interrogate people, and a shudder drives its way through me. He glances at me, obviously pleased to exact some twisted sort of justice on those who dared try to take something of his. I should try to stop him, at least attempt to stifle his rage, but something stops me. A sliver of venomous rage splits me, creating a chasm between what I know is right—what I know to be just—and the unrelenting need to see the men who hurt my son drawn and quartered. Peter's eyes meet mine, and for a moment, he looks pensive. I let the rage fill my expression and he, recognizing it immediately, mercilessly smiles.

I release Paul to the plump nurse, who shuffles in as Peter takes his leave. Grigori offers his hand and I take it, pulling myself to my feet. "The people responsible were Dutch, are you certain?" I ask, wiping my face with my sleeve.

He nods. "At least one, Your Majesty."

The last bit of anger boils away, replaced by suspicion. Would he truly be capable of something like this? Once I would have said no, but the man is so far from the boy I once knew, I sometimes feel as if I don't know him at all.

Squaring my shoulders, I tilt my chin up. "I need to see Alexander, *immediately*."

Chapter

ELEVEN

Alexander is in the library, which doesn't surprise me. There was a time that seeing him here, in a place where we share so many memories, would be a balm to my heart. But when I enter, he looks at me blankly, with the eyes of a stranger. Perhaps I deserve the coolness between us. But I don't have it in me to dwell on it today. Too many other grievances have piled onto the pyre in the past days.

"I summoned you, and you refused me," I accuse as I sweep into the room in a swish of skirts.

"I'm quite busy. I do have a role here besides being your whipping boy." He pauses, seeming to gather himself. "Your Majesty."

"What do you know about a Danish plot against the crown?" I ask flatly and with no further preamble.

Alexander blinks, setting his book on the desk and rubbing his eyes before answering. "What?"

"My son was kidnapped in the village yesterday.

At least one of the men was Danish. Peter is questioning them now. If you know something, I suggest you tell me now, before he slices it out of them himself."

I watch as he flinches. Alexander has never had the stomach for violence. It used to be one of the things I loved about him. And if I'm being completely honest, it is one of the things I love still.

"No, of course not." He looks genuinely affronted. "How could you think such a thing?"

I clasp my hands in front of me, fighting to keep them from shaking. "As envoy to Denmark, if Peter even suspects you have any involvement, he won't hesitate to have you executed."

He stares at me, openmouthed. "And you? Do you really think me capable of harming a child, your child?"

Once, I wouldn't have hesitated, but there is too much between us now. "I know I hurt you. I know you must hate me."

Alexander stands, his eyes level with mine. "I would not take out my pain on an innocent child. And I don't hate you. It would be easier if I did."

"Yet this is your man, if there is anything left of him when Peter finishes his interrogation. I want you to speak to him. Find out why—who is targeting my family."

His expression is cold as he responds. "Of course, Your Majesty."

And with that, he turns and leaves me alone in the room, the smell of stale books thick in the air.

The following week, Peter announces a masked ball. The palace is buzzing with excitement for the first time in ages. For those who had served under Elizabeth, they have grown accustomed to such lavish events happening nearly every night. Peter, by contrast, seems content to stay in his room and drink with his handful of comrades as some of the women from the village dance for their coins.

I doubt I will be able to attend until Dash brings me a special tea made of mint leaves and ginger. Though the taste is rancid, it soothes my sour stomach.

"My mother's recipe," she explains proudly. "It helped me through my pregnancies."

By the time afternoon comes I'm feeling well enough to eat, feeling more like my old self than I have in some time.

Trunks filled with elaborate masks and costumes are brought in and my ladies claw through them like hawks, hunting for just the perfect ensemble. Blood-red ribbons and roses hang from every doorway and wrap every candelabrum. Servants scrub the parquet floors with buckets of soap and rose water, making the entire palace smell like spring. Lanterns are strewn through the gardens and terrace, and a German orchestra can be heard tuning their violins from everywhere in the palace. It's as if someone breathed fresh life into the halls. People are chipper and merry as I pass down the hall, taking everything in. The cook and her staff are busy preparing fresh pheasant and lamb—two of Peter's favorites—and the scent is like heaven on the air.

My seamstress creates a stunning gown of blue and green silk adorned with bright peacock feathers but in the end, it's too gaudy for my taste and I give it to Dash instead, choosing a stark-white gown with a long, swan-head tiara for myself. A ring of white feathers wraps around my neck, tickling me whenever I move. My hair is powdered white and curled, setting tall upon my head with bits of feather poking out here and there. Sergei offers to escort me to the ball, but I know Peter will be watching me very closely, so I politely refuse, choosing Dash and two of my other ladies as escorts instead. When I arrive at the top of the grand staircase and the herald announces me, all eyes turn toward me, and as heads bow, I begin my descent.

Again, Peter has failed to leave me a seat. However, when I approach the head table, Prince George stands, humbly offering me his chair, which earns him a menacing glare from Peter. Elizavetta fans herself with a scrap of red lace, and for the life of me, I can't put together what her costume is. Her gown is red, dark at the bottom and growing lighter as it crawls up her waist and across her ample chest. Her elbow-length gloves are cut from similar cloth, and are far too tight, making her arms protrude from the top like two sausages. Her lips are painted deep burgundy and her hair is piled atop her head. If anything, it looks less orange than usual, and more the color of fire. Then I see it. Two tiny, red horns poking out from the mass of hair.

She's a devil.

It's almost funny enough to set me into a fit of laughter. Beside me, Dash must see the same thing because she chortles, covering the noise with a delicate cough.

Taking my seat, I carefully pick at my food. I'm trying to enjoy the music despite the fact that Peter is feeding Elizavetta off his fork and laughing rambunctiously when a bit of meat falls into her cleavage and he is forced to retrieve it by sticking his face into her bodice.

For his part, Peter makes no secret of his plans to divorce me, and all eyes turn in my direction sympathetically every time he alludes to it.

"See, my lovely Romanova, my delicate flower," he says, running a finger down Elizavetta's exposed shoulder. She chuckles, stands, and waves her hand across the assembly as if lording over them.

"My first order of business, as your new queen, will be... to drink more wine!" she spits, raising her cup and sloshing the contents. A small laugh runs through the room, though I'm entirely sure they are laughing at her rather than with her.

Once the meal is finished, Peter leads the assembly to the throne room, taking his seat with a flourish. He's brought in a small side chair to sit beside his on the pedestal, which Elizavetta falls onto without hesitation. Once more, all eyes swing to me and I make a show of climbing the few steps and folding myself gracefully onto the floor to Peter's other side.

Once everyone has filed in, Peter stands, clapping his hands once. "I have gathered you together to witness a momentous occasion." The crowd hushes. "This week, my son and heir was taken by those who would seek to destabilize our beloved country. Those men have been executed. But before their deaths, it was discovered that one of them had ties to Danish court."

I watch in horror as his eyes lock on to Alexander in the crowd. "While I cannot prove he was acting on orders from the Danish king, I have decided that a show of force is necessary. And so this week, I am dispatching troops to Demark. We will take the country, and any who oppose us will be razed to the ground." He lifts a glass as if to toast, but the room is silent.

I stand, leaning over and whispering. "Peter, you can't declare war on Denmark with no evidence.

They are our ally. If you attack them unprovoked—"
I don't get to finish my thought. His hand shoots out,
slapping me in the face so hard I pitch forward and
roll down the small staircase.

My ears are still ringing when he slowly climbs
down and takes a handful of my hair in his fist, lifting me to my feet. I make a strangled noise, but I
manage to keep from crying out, though my eyes
water from the sting.

He sweeps a glance around the room. "There
may be some of you who question my decisions. But
I am sovereign Russia. This country, and everyone
in it, belongs to me. I decide who we will be at war
with, and I will decide who to call my wife."

He's shouting now, spittle flying from his mouth
as he takes two steps forward, dragging me with
him. When he finally releases me, I stumble but
manage to keep my feet under me.

"George, take her to the cells!"

I blink, steeling myself to be taken into custody.
But to my surprise, George doesn't move. He simply
lowers his head.

"Mikhail!" Peter yells, looking for support from
his oldest friend. Mikhail rushes to Peter's side and
furiously whispers. Peter waves him off in an angry
fit.

"Guards, take her!" he orders. Two guards near
the rear door move, only to be met with a line of
nobles blocking their path. My own guards rush in,

swords drawn, and circle me.

I can feel the rage radiating off Peter in waves. Straightening myself, I hold up my hands. "No, please. Let them through." Then to Grigori, "Let them take me; that is my command."

Reluctantly, the nobles step aside and my guards retreat. But before his guards can touch me, Peter screams and they freeze. "No! You will not obey her. You will obey me!"

For a long moment, no one moves. Battle lines have been drawn, and it's as if the entire assembly might erupt into a bloody massacre right here in open court. My breath is coming too fast, I realize, forcing myself to still against the rising panic. Unsure what else to do to defuse the situation, I turn to Peter and curtsy deeply.

"Yes, we will obey our king!" I say, my voice as steady as I can make it. Around me, others do the same, some even dropping to one knee.

Finally, Peter takes a deep breath, seeming to calm. But it's a menacing sound, one I know all too well, and goose bumps break out across my skin. It's the sound the wind makes before it blows—the sound of waves an instant before they crash to the shore. The sound of inevitability. While I realize that nothing can stop him now, I know I must try anyway. I must attempt to contain the damage.

"Punish me, if you will, but leave the others. It was only their deep sense of chivalry that drove them to defend me, nothing more," I plead.

The side of his mouth curls up as Peter nods. "Yes, you must be punished. You publically challenged my authority, and your punishment will be equally public."

I swallow hard. A flogging, if I'm lucky. Or perhaps simply a few days in the stockade. He will punish me, but he will not kill me, not even for this. I sag, a moment of relief washing over me, but he sees it, and in his eyes, I see something change.

Moving slowly across the room, he grabs a crystal flask of liquid, each step, each gesture, exaggerated like a court fool might. When he moves back to me, he holds it close enough for me to smell, swirling the clear liquid inside. Vodka? My confusion lasts only a moment.

"An example must be made," he continues.

Slowly, he begins pouring it down my shoulders, into my hair, and down my white, feathered gown. The liquid is cold against my hot flesh, soaking into the heavy damask and crinoline. The heavy odor fills my lungs, making each breath sting. Around me, people watch, looks of shock and horror etched onto their faces. I find Sergei in the crowd and hold his gaze. His blue-green eyes are narrowed, his hand hovering inches above the long knife attached to his waistcoat. I shake my head, imperceptibly, and he blinks, still not relaxing. He's trying to decide if he's going to come to my rescue, but I know that if he does, Peter will kill us both. His jaw clenches, but finally, he drops his hand. I feel myself relax, just a bit, as Peter begins speaking again, drawing my attention to his face. He's excited, like a child about to play his favorite game. It's then that the real fear hits me.

"My aunt didn't believe in executing her enemies. She understood that death was a privilege, that there were far worse things." He pauses, sweeping the room with a glance. "Let me be very clear. I will not tolerate any disloyalty." He replaces the now-empty flask on the tray and picks up a lit candle from the nearby candelabra. I hold his gaze as he walks slowly toward me, each footstep echoing in the deathly still room. The pulse beats in my ears so loudly it drowns out all other sounds, my heart fluttering in my ribcage like a hummingbird. I will not let him see me afraid, I decide, steeling myself. I will not give him the pleasure. I would rather die in flames right now than to let him break me again. Lifting my chin, I refuse to falter.

Once he's close enough, he leans in close, whispering into my ear. "I have wanted to do this for a very long time, wife."

He touches the flame to my gown. All I can do is scream as chaos erupts around me.

Chapter

TWELVE

The flames lick up my gown, catching into my hair, the smell of burnt hair and feathers suffocating me as I continue to scream. I fumble with the laces of my gown, but I can't reach them. I'm barely aware of the other screams, of the nobles and guests rushing from the room. Behind me, Peter is yelling for them to watch, to watch me burn as a witch should. Then he laughs. The sound of it rolls through me, mixing with the fire and the pain. Hands are on me, some patting out the fire with bare skin, others fumbling to help me shed the cloth. The fabric is falling from me in flaming strips, yet I still can't free myself. Even as I'm writhing, fighting to keep the flames off my face, I feel the first burns on my flesh, on my back, my arms, and my neck. It's a blinding pain, one that drives all reason away.

The next thing I know, someone is ripping the remnants of my dress off me, tossing it aside. Hands press wet cloth to my head and neck, somehow both soothing and upsetting the burns. I scream, but I can't move. I'm not crying, there's far too much anger and fear for that, but I'm shaking all over. Pairs of arms cradle me. Opening my eyes, I see that Sergei, Alexander, and Grigori are all holding me, cocooned safely in their arms. I can barely see Peter, but I do see Mikhail holding him back as he rages. There are other hands now, lifting, carrying, helping me from the room into the hall. I'm nothing but pain; everything else has been burned away. When they touch me, I cry out, but they must get me out of the room. Some distant piece of my mind knows that. Soon, the pain becomes too much and the darkness wraps me in sweet, blissful oblivion.

I don't remember making it to my room, but I register the feel of gentle hands peeling the last of the melted fabric from my body, and then lifting me into a tub of cool water. At first, it hurts, the burns are raw and the water is like a million bee stings, forcing my consciousness back into my body, but then I let myself settle into it, the pain fading into something close to pleasure—relief. Someone else is in the water too, pouring the cool liquid over my shoulders and chest. Another set of hands is working fingers through my hair, pressing a damp cloth to my face. I know their touches without opening my eyes.

My men—my hearts.

When I can finally breathe again, my eyes flutter open and I'm staring up into Alexander's warm, dark eyes. Behind me, I hear Sergei humming softly, a tune both foreign and familiar, like something out of a dream. Dash bursts into the room with a jar of oil they pour in the water and gently rub into my skin. I murmur thanks and she slowly backs away, leaving me to my rescuers. Alexander, still clothed in his midnight blue costume suit, kneels in the basin at my feet, massaging the oil into my legs. Rolling my head back, I catch sight of Sergei doing the same for my neck and shoulders. The oil begins to numb my skin, drawing the last of the flames from my body. It tingles, a cool, refreshing tickle. Sighing deeply, I relax against the back of the copper tub, just relishing their gentle touches.

Now, their faces twin masks of concern and love, they are as radiant as God's own angels. Deep inside me, the rage subsides, giving way to a stranger, stronger feeling, a need I cannot quite explain. My hands float in the water, shaking hard enough to create ripples in the surface.

The shaking intensifies until I'm an earthquake, my body wracked with spasm after spasm. All I can feel is the want, the pulling need to draw them to me and never let them go. Pushing forward through the water, I press myself into Alexander's arms. He hesitates only a fraction of a moment before submitting, before relaxing against me. But even his embrace isn't enough to fill the cavernous need inside me. Reaching back, I grab Sergei by the shirt, dragging him into the water with us. Once I feel him against my back, something inside me purrs contentedly. The shaking subsides as both men wrap their arms around me. If it's strange or awkward, I can't feel it. I can't feel anything beyond the familiar ridges of their bodies. Sergei lowers his head and kisses my shoulder, my hair, my ear. I'm on fire again, only this time, it's a good burn, a healing burn, if such a thing exists. The last remnants of fear and doubt are scorched from existence.

Alexander rests his head against mine, murmuring. "I'm so sorry. I love you. I love you. Can you forgive me?"

Reaching up, I graze his bottom lip with my fingers and he kisses them reverently.

As I turn to look over my shoulder, Sergei sees my unspoken demand and leans in, kissing me hard on the mouth, our lips locking until I can't breathe, until I'm drowning in him. When he releases me, Alexander tips my chin to him and does the same. He tries to pull back but I grab him by the back of the neck, holding the kiss until my lungs scream for air.

Finally, Sergei stands, stepping from the deep tub, his clothes dripping onto the marble floor. Reaching down, he lifts me from the water as if I'm completely weightless. Alexander follows as he carries me to my room, setting me gently on the bed. My skin tingles in the breeze from the open window and, despite my nakedness, I feel completely safe. Alexander lights the bedside lamp, illuminating the room in a soft, golden glow. Crawling onto the bed behind me, Sergei begins brushing out my hair, the wet drops falling like rain down my bare back. Alexander moves in front of me, stripping off his soaking jacket and shirt to reveal his bare, muscular chest. Slowly, he kneels, his eyes locked on mine. He kisses one knee, and then the other, his lips tracing their way up my thighs as I arch my back in anticipation.

Sergei's body vanishes for a minute, making me mewl desperately. When he returns to my back, his body is as naked as my own. He wraps his hands around me, cupping my bare breasts in his powerful hands.

They are mine, my sun and my moon, the best and worst parts of me, my strength and my weakness, my mortal sin and my fatal flaw. I draw them against me, needing them as I need air in my lungs, aching for them in ways I never imagined possible.

I fall into them, into the melding of flesh and souls. For these few hours of flesh and kisses and driving passion, it feels as if the world is mine, as if nothing bad can touch me and everything I've ever wanted is mine for the taking.

The morning comes in a haze. I sit up in bed, still nude as the day I was born, and sore all over. I look myself over. The burns are red and angry. There are no blisters that I can see, but when my sheets graze the marks, I flinch in pain. I wonder for a moment if my memories of last night were real, or a pain-induced dream. I wonder how, after what Peter has done, I can wake up feeling so calm and secure. But more than anything, I wonder what strange turn my life will take next.

Dash knocks on my door before peeking her head in. "Your Highness, are you ready to dress? I've sent for some coffee."

I wave her in, feeling more chipper than I have any right to after Peter's escapade. After applying another vial of oil to calm my burns, we dress slowly, each layer of cloth rubbing raw against my tender flesh, and when I turn to the mirror, my reflection shocks me. My hair, my long, ebony black hair, is matted and gnarled up to my shoulders. I touch it, and brittle balls of melted hair fall into my hand.

"Don't worry; I'm sure Jean can repair it," Dash offers with a weak smile.

I wordlessly nod. It's not so much my hair that bothers me, but the fact that Peter has finally shown his true colors to the masses. No one will support his insanity now. People will be desperate to be free of him, painting even more of a target on not just Peter's own head, but on tiny Paul's as well.

There's no choice now. For the first time, the path ahead of me is as clear as midday. To keep myself, my country, and my son safe, I'm going to have to rally forces against my husband.

The thought curls tight knots into my stomach, but when I step into my outer chamber, I'm stunned. Flowers, gifts, and letters of well wishes in the wake of Peter's outburst fill the room until the odor, the sickly sweet bouquet of hundreds of flowers, is nearly overpowering.

"Dash, make a list of everyone who sent a gift or a letter. I will want to personally thank each of them," I order, stepping through the maze of gifts.

She nods and settles me into the vanity chair before rushing off for paper and a quill. Jean enters the room, and though he tries to hide it, his dismay at my state is plain on his face. He bows, recovering himself before opening his trunk of brushes and irons.

He pulls out a pair of sheers like one might use on a lamb.

"It's quite uneven, Your Highness. I think it best we even it out before we begin."

"Whatever you can do, Jean."

He nods, biting down on his bottom lip before hacking away. When he's finished, the line of hair is well above my shoulders, but smooth and straight.

"I can add bits of wig," he offers.

I shake my head. "No, let it be. I want people to

see what Peter has done. I will not hide from it. It is his shame to bear, not my own."

He nods. Taking two strands from each side, he skillfully pulls the strands back and braids them through my hair, leaving the back straight. He adds a few jeweled combs and my tiara. If anything, having the hair back and off my shoulders draws the eye to my long, narrow chin, to my deep-set brown eyes, and my high cheekbones.

Behind me, he clasps his hands in admiration of his good work, and I offer him a warm smile.

"Thank you, Jean. It's lovely."

Dash returns, paper in hand. "I've compiled your list, Your Highness."

I nod, standing and brushing my hands down my green satin bodice. An ache ripples up my arms as the fabric brushes the tender, burned skin, and I have to fight back a wince. "Good. But the first thing I must do is make myself seen. My people must know I am well. They must see that I am not diminished by Peter's cruelty."

Dash curtsies and snaps her fingers to the maids scurrying around the room. "Gather the other ladies-in-waiting. Her Highness wishes to take a formal stroll through the palace."

Once my entire entourage arrives, we set out. Every move is agony, every step like sandpaper on my skin as the dress brushes my legs, yet I conceal it, forcing my mind past the pain. Thinking of the bath helps, distracts me from the discomfort. First, we take a stroll through the gardens, the brilliant fountains spitting water high into the air as we pass by, creating a cool mist on my face. Then we move to the council chambers, where I greet several of the higher nobility, each of whom is elated to see me so undamaged. We attend a picnic lunch in the open air balcony, and then I make an appearance in the throne room. Pausing outside to be announced, I steady myself so that when the doors open, I stride in with my chin high, my shoulders back, and a hint of a smile on my face as I glide past the assembly. Peter is sitting on the throne, looking half asleep until he sees me, then he rights himself, glaring in my direction. I approach, curtsying to him briefly before taking my spot at his side. Neither of us speaks, but the chill between us is unmistakable. Finally, after several minutes of listening to Lord Grey make his case for adding troops to the western border, Peter yawns.

"I cannot spare forces at the moment. I am readying my invasion force to leave within the week."

Lord Grey's eyes shift to me, and then to his own feet. "Yes, Your Highness."

"I have men to spare," I say loudly. Peter swings his head in my direction, but I don't spare him a look. "I have two dozen Russian Imperial soldiers, displaced by the new house guard, and given to me by my husband as my personal guard. They may lack some traits found in His Highness' Holstein soldiers, but I think they will serve you well in the protection of your lands."

Lord Grey looks up, as if waiting in fear of Peter's reprisal. I swing my chin toward Peter, silently challenging him with my expression. "It would not do to let one of our lords fear for the borders of his own land. Don't you agree, Peter?"

I add his name as an afterthought, a slight in retribution for the evening before. It's a risk, challenging him so openly. Perhaps he will retaliate as he did last night, but I am feeling reckless, invincible. And I know that I must prove my willingness to stand up to him if I have any hope of garnering real support from the nobles. *Let him attack me again,* I think. This time, I will be prepared. This time, I will have him slaughtered like Caesar on the ides of March.

He stares at me for a moment, then, possibly seeing his fate in my eyes, he sits back, waving his hand. "Then the matter is settled."

The day proceeds without my having to intervene again, and toward the end of court, Peter begins leaning toward me, asking for my counsel. It's a shift that registers in the face of everyone present, a small victory I know I will need.

By the time I retire to my room to prepare for supper, I'm exhausted and my skin is on fire and itching like the devil. Dash takes the time to help me apply more oil to the burns before dressing me for dinner. At exactly eight o'clock, both Sergei and Alexander arrive to escort me to the dining chamber. They chat pleasantly enough as Dash adjusts my hair and reapplies my makeup. I watch them in the reflection of my mirror, flushing at the memory of the night before.

Sergei sits, his jacket the dark green of a Russian general, ribbons and medals hanging from his chest. His dark hair is combed back, giving an illusion that it is much shorter than it is. Alexander, by contrast, is wearing a sky-blue tunic and breeches that make his dark hair and eyes stand out even more than usual. He's freshly shaven, and his cheeks rosy as he laughs at something Sergei has said.

"Dash, can you leave us for a moment?" I ask. She bobs into a deep curtsy and leaves the room. I walk to my men, kissing each of them in turn. Turning my back to Sergei, I hold my hand out to Alexander, who steps forward to take it.

"Before we go, there is something I must tell you," I begin slowly. His face falls into a look of panic for only a moment before righting itself. I glance over my shoulder at Sergei, who nods in encouragement. "You see," I pause, unsure how to begin. "I realized not long ago that I am with child. With your child."

His mouth falls open just a fraction as he glances from Sergei to me and back again. "Were you planning on telling me this?" he asks, his voice barely a whisper, giving no insight into how he must be feeling.

I bite my lip before answering. "I was, but then we had that terrible fight and... I didn't want to force your decision. I wanted to give you space and time to heal. But yes, I would have told you eventually either way."

For a terrible moment, I'm afraid he's truly angry. But he blinks and, reaching out, cups his palms over my belly. "Our child," he mutters.

I smile. "Yes, my love. Our child."

With a sound that can only be a cry of joy, he pulls me into his arms, pressing me along the length of him.

"But there is a complication," Sergei warns, drawing us apart. "Peter must never know about the pregnancy. He will know there is no way the child is his."

I watch Alexander's face as he works through what Sergei is saying.

Sergei continues. "It would give Peter all the grounds he needs for a divorce, or worse."

Alexander takes a deep breath. "What is your solution then?"

"I will hide my condition. Sergei will find someone to take the child after it's born, take it to safety, perhaps in the north." I pause, resting my hands on my stomach. "And then, I am going to lead a coup against Peter. It's become very clear to me that he puts himself, and the whole of Russia, in danger with his incompetence. He will not hear reason. I have tried, but I cannot allow it to continue. He must be deposed, for the good of us all."

"And then, you can bring our child home?" Alexander asks hopefully.

I press my lips together. "Yes. Once it's safe, once Peter is gone, I will bring him home to us."

Chapter

THIRTEEN

Peter doesn't show up at dinner, leaving me to not only sit at the head of the table in his place, but to make a further show of my quick wit while entertaining the assembly. There's a lightness to the room, the deep sense of foreboding that hovers like a storm cloud over Peter's head is noticeably absent. *It could always be like this,* is my silent message to them. *Follow me and I can drive away the darkness from our lives.*

The next week, I begin my self-imposed seclusion. I only venture from my chamber when Peter is out visiting nearby lands, and I am always careful to conceal my fragile condition. I barely develop a hint of a stomach until well into my seventh month, and that is easily enough hidden under the formal Russian caftan jackets I begin to wear. My message is that I am of Russia, that following me will lead them away from Peter's dangerous alliance with Prussia, and not into another one. Soon, they have all but forgotten my humble beginnings and have fully accepted me as one of their own.

My private meetings go well, with no less than two dozen lords firmly on my side, many of whom possess private armies of their own, and the entirety of the Russian army ready to follow at my command. My days are spent in meetings, discussing strategy and preparations, but my nights I spend with the ones I love. Sometimes individually, sometimes together, but they are restorative to my soul. No matter how tired or weak I feel, I can rest in their arms and know that all is right.

A great deal of my time is spent at the cathedral, taking the Blessed Sacrament or in silent prayer. I no longer pray for forgiveness for my sins, but in gratitude for all that I have been given. The clergy and Synod take every opportunity to offer blessings upon me, and I know that they, too, will support me when the time comes. It's Peter's own cruelty toward the church that has lost him their support, that and by so openly abusing his wife and co-regent, he has transgressed beyond the point of redemption—as if such a thing mattered to him.

After leaving the chapel, I decide to walk back to the palace. My guards hover around me, though Grigori is off meeting with troops in Moscow at my behest and I feel his absence like a thorn in my side. Beside me, Sergei walks slowly, the afternoon sun casting shadows across his face. The air grows cold, the familiar bite of autumn nipping at my nose as we walk down the street. Sergei looks much the same as the day I met him, his tall, black fur hat covering his hair and ears, a rugged line of stubble along his chin and cheeks. He takes a deep breath and absently rubs at his whiskers.

"What is it, Sergei?" I ask, knowing the pensive expression all too well.

He replies in low, somber tones. "I believe I have found a family to take the child. They are loyal to you and can take the child to Denmark as soon as it is delivered."

I have to force myself not to touch the small lump hidden beneath my fur jacket. Inside me there is a twisting feeling I've been able to push away until now. The child will come soon, and my plan will roll into motion. I've been so focused on the details, all save this one thing. The thought is simply too painful to bear.

"Peter will be back from Riga within the week. How on earth will we keep the birth a secret?" I ask, nervousness fluttering in my stomach.

"I will think of something," he says confidently, pausing long enough to offer me a sidelong glance.

Suddenly, I cannot get back to the palace quickly enough.

As the days once again grow short, I decide

I must visit Paul whilst I'm still able. He's far too young to understand that soon I will be unable to make my weekly visits. It will be too difficult to hide my quickly growing condition. In my hands, I clutch a box of puppets I've had made for him, a humble offering for a young prince who wants for nothing. Rina's son has joined him in the royal nursery. He's a dark-haired, soft-spoken child—a steep contrast to Paul's white-blond curls and devious grin.

Paul is quickly becoming the bane of his nurses, though I doubt any of them would admit as much. I visit him every Sunday, if only to sit in the nursery and read to myself while he plays. Last week, he threw a tantrum when one of his favorite wooden soldiers broke, heaving it at his nurse and hitting her in the face. She looked to me, perhaps in hope that I would chastise him on her behalf. I was too startled to say anything. It was much like watching a tiny version of my husband, and I was stricken with grief at the spectacle.

Now, as I approach the nursery, a familiar sense of dread sets in. The valet opens the door, and my heart sinks into my chest. There, sitting on the floor, are Peter and Elizavetta. I stride in, unable to keep the clipped tone from my voice. "Peter, what are you doing here?" I demand.

It's Elizavetta who answers. "We brought the boy some toys and a new uniform."

She tugs at the bright blue Prussian jacket enveloping my son. Her expression is one of pure maliciousness.

Stepping between them, I grab Paul by the arm, lugging him from her grasp. Dropping to my knees, I rip the jacket from his small body, tossing it across the floor. "Paul is a Prince of Russia; I would thank you not to forget that," I order, glaring at the nurses who stand against the far wall, looking on helplessly.

Peter stands, brushing himself off. "He is my son, and so he is a Duke of Holstein. And considering your own humble beginnings, I'd say he's more Prussian than Russian by any account."

When I turn on him, I fear for a moment that I might rip his throat out like a mother lion defending her cub. "You idiot! He's already been taken once by those who fear your love for Prussia over Russia. Do you think by filling his head with this that you are making him safe? You are making him a target, Peter, and I will not stand for it."

He opens his mouth to speak, and I silence him with a glare. "Do not think to test me on this, Peter. I will do whatever it takes to protect my son."

Now Elizavetta stands, wobbly and unbalanced as she rises in her wide pannier skirt. "How dare you speak to your king in such a tone! He could have you whipped..."

Taking two strides forward, I come nose to nose with her. "And have you told him yet that it was you who pushed me down the stairs? That it was you who caused the death of our first child? If there's a punishment to be handed out, I should think you would be the one on the receiving end."

At my accusation, Peter steps back, looking back and forth between us. If she is concerned about his wrath, it doesn't show. Her expression remains unchanged. "You have no proof."

Though I never saw her face, I have always known the truth. "I assure you, I'd recognize your stench anywhere," I spit back.

Without waiting for her to speak again, Peter takes her by the arm, half-dragging her from the room. Though the valet closes the door behind them, I can hear his angry screams and her high-pitched rebuttals. When I finally look back down at Paul, he's sitting cross-legged on the floor, sobbing quietly. I kneel down to comfort him, but he darts away, skittering across the floor and clutching the skirts of his nurse.

"I'm so sorry, Paul. I didn't mean to upset you," I offer in a feather-light tone. Pushing the box across the floor, I smile. "I've brought you a present."

He stares at me for a minute, then shakes his head and buries his face in the skirts.

A heaviness spreads through me like hot lead. He hates me. Of course he does. Perhaps he can sense my own hesitation toward him. When I finally leave the nursery, I'm crying too. Sergei bumps into me in the hall as I make my way back to my chamber.

"What's wrong?" he asks, hesitant to openly console me.

Wiping my eyes, I frown. "It shouldn't be this hard to love your own child," I listlessly respond. "But I see so much of Peter in him. So much brutality."

"Perhaps you need to look deeper," he suggests.

I don't answer. Truthfully, I don't want to look any deeper. I'm too afraid of what I'll find.

Chapter

FOURTEEN

The labor pains begin early in the morning, only a few weeks later. I know from experience how long the ordeal may be, but I call for Sergei and Alexander immediately. Truthfully, I'm afraid. Sergei kisses me quickly, and then takes his leave, fetching Vasily, my personal valet and one of the few people who knows of our plan. I pace the floor in my inner chamber, Alexander holding my hand as I walk. He's nervous—as any expectant father might be, but there's another fear we share. The best-made plans too often fail, and in this, we will have only one chance. He recites writings of a man named Voltaire, who he considers a sage of our time. I have to say, a few pages in and I'm mesmerized by his thinking. He speaks in ways both plain and metaphorical. I know I want to meet him, when all this comes to an end, and I ask Dash to draft an invitation. If I survive the next few days, I'll send it. If not…

Well, best not to think of that as I rally my strength.

Dash sends messages to my ladies and maids that I've taken ill and won't likely be seen for a few days until it has passed. The physician comes by, but she tells him it's simply symptoms of my monthly courses, and he flees without further question.

We dare not send for the court midwife, so rather, I ask for Vasily's wife, Gerta, and my dear friend Madame Groot to be present. They both have some experience in these matters, and I'm confident they can assist me well enough. I continue to pace and when the pain becomes too much, Madame Groot begins to loudly play the piano to hide my soft cries.

Time moves slowly and quickly in unison, though I'm not sure how it's possible. By the time dusk arrives, I can no longer walk. My back aches and my feet are sore. It's then that I hear the wails coming from the town just outside the palace walls. Even from my bed, I can smell the soot, the burning tinder. Alexander kisses my forehead, then rushes off to find Peter and lure him to the town to watch the blaze. Vasily has set his own home, and a nearby stable, aflame. The idea is to draw everyone from the palace—either to watch or to assist in quenching the fire before it spreads out of control. It's a risk, for certain, but we are left with little alternative.

Dash returns a few moments later. "Your Highness, the palace is nearly empty. Everyone has gone to town."

I exhale slowly, taking Gerta by her plump hand.

She's in a simple grey dress, a white apron, and her brown hair is tied back from her face with a scrap of blue ribbon. "I'm so sorry for your home," I mutter, knowing I'm on the verge of incoherency. "I will send you with enough gold to buy a new home in Denmark."

She nods and pats my hand. We have discussed all this before. She and Vasily are leaving tomorrow to take their poor, orphaned nephew to Denmark after a fire destroys their home here in Russia. From there, they will hand the child over to Alexander's cousin in Bobriki, who will raise the child as his own until he can be brought safely home.

I assume it will be a boy, of course. Women in my position know all too well the value of producing sons. But a daughter would be lovely. A wispy little princess with ebony hair and sea green eyes...

As soon as I conjure the image in my mind, it's driven away by the pain and I lie back on the bed of linens they have spread on the floor for me, and the real labor begins.

The delivery goes quickly and my child, my beautiful son, comes into the world, quiet as a mouse—as even from his first breath, he knows the dangerous world he's been brought into. Gerta wraps him in silver cloth and lays him on my lap. I touch his face with my fingertips, forcing myself to memorize every tiny ridge, every contour, and every perfect slope. My arms ache at the thought of letting him go. My chest constricts and hot tears run down the slope of my nose, splashing onto his pink cheek.

"My beautiful son. I name you Alexei, for your father, Gregorivitch, for the man who secured your safety, and give you the title of Count Bobrinski. My precious son, I hope you can forgive me for what I'm about to do." Kissing his tiny head, I breathe in the scent of him, warm and new, and I know I will never forget it as long as I live. With a shaky breath, I hand my child to Gerta, who smiles sadly at his sleeping face. A small whimper rises up, escaping my lips before I can recapture it.

"I will care for him as if he were my own, Your Highness."

Madame Groot, her hair now silver as the jewels around her slender neck, kisses my temple, and then rises from my side to escort Gerta through the secret door behind my wardrobe. I manage to hold myself together until they are gone, but once the door closes behind them, the torrent releases. Dash gathers me into her arms, rocking me as I sob, reaching through the empty air for my child.

My first child was murdered before he drew his first breath, my second was stolen from me, and my third, I handed away. And although I swore to bring him back when his safety could be assured, some dark place in my heart knows I never will. It will never be safe enough to bring my little Alexei home. Laying back I squeeze my eyes closed, the pain of labor replaced with a new pain, something much deeper and much more permanent.

Deep inside me, another fissure opens in my heart.

Chapter

FIFTEEN

I'm sitting in my chamber when the letter from St. Trudpert monastery in Münstertal arrives. Troops came in the night, looking for the man known as Pigeon. As per my orders, he was not taken alive. The letter is to inform me that he has been interred on monastery grounds. I read the words over and over, burning them into my mind.

Ivan is dead.

On my orders.

I crumble the parchment in my hand, tossing it in the crackling fire. It's been less than two days, but I can wait no longer. This is evidence that Russia's enemies are gathering forces to move against Peter—and by default, me and our son. Trying to take Ivan is a move born of desperation, and desperate men are dangerous men. I don't inquire as to who was behind the attack—it doesn't really matter. Perhaps it was Peter himself, or some foreign power looking for a non-Romanov heir. Either way, the threat has been eliminated.

How cold the words feel in my mind. I have to remind myself that Ivan was more than a threat. He was a person, a lost boy stripped of everything in life simply because of his lineage. What a double-edged sword power can be, both to those who possess it and to those who threaten it.

A tap at my door shakes me from my thoughts. It's Mikhail. I don't stand at his entrance and he bows, looking up at me through thin, stringy, yellow hair. Once, he'd been so handsome, so closely resembling Peter as a young man that one might have thought them brothers. But the years have not been kind and now he stands, hunched, a shell of the man he once was, his hair gone from the front of his head and his face sallow.

"Your Majesty, I thought you should know Peter is about to leave to go inspect his troops at Oranienbaum. Do you wish to accompany him?" he asks.

I feel myself frown. The invitation could not have come from Peter, who has not said a word to me in months. Was this some way for Mikhail to let me know of Peter's plans discreetly? I watch him with wary eyes. Mikhail is clever enough; he must at least suspect what is coming. I know that he would be an asset to me, if only to serve as a watchful eye over Peter once he is deposed.

"I think not. I am quite busy here. But thank you for the kind invitation," I finally say.

He bows again and takes his leave. Turning to Dash, who is quietly sewing in the far corner of the room, I hold up my hand.

"Dash, please fetch Lord Salkov. And is Grigori returned yet?"

She sets her stitching aside, standing. "Only today I believe, Your Majesty. Shall I fetch him as well?"

"Yes, please. And tell the ladies that I'm feeling much better."

With a curtsy, she hurries off to do as I bid. While she's gone, I pull paper and a quill from my desk and settle in to write a letter to the Privy Council. My words are clear. Peter has left the Winter Palace, refusing to be properly crowned and anointed, and has gone to Oranienbaum to inspect more Prussian troops. I say, simply but plainly, that should he remain sovereign, that it is only a matter of short time before he hands Russia over to King Fredrick. I outline my plan to force him to abdicate, leaving me as sovereign Empress of Russia, and I ask for their support. I add that doing so is not treason against the crown, but a necessary step toward protecting the nation and preserving the crown that serves it. With blood-red wax, I affix my personal emblem, sealing not just my letter but my fate as well.

There can be no turning back now.

Two days later, I'm requested to attend the council. Rather than a gown, I choose to wear a traditional Russian military uniform, green ushanka, a matching riding skirt, and my red Order of St. Catherine Ribbon draped across my chest. When I arrive, silence cuts through the room like a sword. I stride in, unabashed, and take a seat in the golden throne of Imperial Russia.

"My lords, you requested my presence?"

Lord Grey is the first to step forward. Without preamble, he drops to one knee, his fist over his chest. Soon, others do the same until there is no one standing in the room. Even Alexander and Sergei are kneeling in fealty.

I stand. "Your support is recognized and appreciated. I will ride out today with my personal army and meet Peter in Oranienbaum. There, I will convince him to abdicate the throne to me. When I return, I will greet the council and Synod in the Fortress of Peter and Paul and be formally recognized. Afterwards, I will return to the Winter Palace and address the crowd from the main balcony, along with my son and heir Paul." I pause, looking around the room, the weight of my actions resting like heavy stones upon my shoulders. "Now rise, my privy council, and greet your empress."

They obey, and I exit the room to thunderous applause. The same applause, I recall clearly, that greeted Peter upon his ascension to the throne not so long ago. A lump forms in my throat, and I fight to swallow it down as I make my way to the stable.

Chapter

SIXTEEN

The ride to Oranienbaum is a slow, arduous one. I have to stop periodically to change the bandages I still wear from giving birth not one week ago. The closer we get to my old home, the more my muscles tighten into stone, the more my throat dries out, and the more my old doubts and fears fight to creep into the back of my thoughts. Still, with my guard at my back, and Sergei and Alexander at my sides, I press on.

"I don't think it's wise to keep Mikhail as chancellor," Sergei says again, as though perhaps I hadn't heard him the twice before.

"He is clever and well liked by the Synod. He has often spoken in my defense against Peter."

"Then why does he not stand with you now?" he demands. "He is a coward, playing both sides until a clear victor is decided. He will be trouble, I promise you."

I sigh. "Or is it just that you had your own eye on the position?" As soon as I speak the words, I regret them.

"Of course not."

Alexander cuts in. "Then what positions shall we have? Or are we simply to remain in court as the empress' mistresses?"

Rolling my head to the side, I crack the bones in my neck. "I will find you suitable appointments, of course. Though if you continue pressing me on the matter, you both might end up as the court stolniks."

"I'm merely pointing out that there are more trustworthy men to place at your side," Sergei finally says.

"I find trust a rare commodity, especially in men. I seem to have the last two trustworthy men in Russia riding beside me." I turn, glancing over my shoulder at Grigori, who rides a chestnut stallion a few paces back. "Well, the last three at any rate."

Upon our arrival at Oranienbaum, we come across a small force of Holstein guards just outside the palace grounds. Sergei motions for me to stay back, but I ignore him, riding to the front lines. The time for meekness has passed. I will succeed or die trying. And if I am to fall this day, I'd rather it be with an army at my back and a sword in my hand. Drawing my weapon, I ride ahead of the regiment, into the middle of the confused-looking soldiers.

"Men! You may know me. I am Empress Catherine. Only today, the Council of Lords and the Synod gave me their blessing to come here and deliver a message to Peter, to tell him that I am God's chosen ruler in Russia. I do not seek to harm any of you, but if you draw arms against me, if you stand in my way, I will unleash the fury of my army upon you. So before you raise your sword, consider my words and know that I speak for Russia."

After a few confused moments, one solitary man draws his sword, only to be quickly and unceremoniously knocked out by a fellow soldier. Tugging on the reins, I rear Peony onto her back legs. Around me, like a wave on the ocean, men collapse to their knees.

Cheers of "Long Live Queen Catherine!" and "All Hail the Queen!" echo across the field like a song. With a wave of my arm, I send my soldiers forward past me and onto the main palace grounds.

While I wait on horseback, my lieutenants make the first sweep of the palace, only to find it empty. Beneath me, Peony shuffles skittishly in the dying afternoon light.

"Someone must have warned him we were coming," Grigori reports. "From the tracks, I'd say they left not two hours past."

I curse. Of course. Hated as he was, Peter would still have at least one loyal ally in court. "Where have they gone?" I ask, sounding more irritated than I intend.

"South, judging from the trail. Probably heading for Riga in search of allies. Perhaps he's even heading to Prussia."

I turn to Sergei. "If he makes it out of Russia, Fredrick will shield him, and my bid for the throne will be lost."

Sergei nods, spurring his horse to turn to face the soldiers. "There's no time to be lost. Water the horses quickly and gather any supplies we may need. We will have to pursue into the night."

He turns back to me. "What shall we do with Peter's soldiers?"

"They will join my army," I order.

"Are you certain that's wise? They are Prussians, after all."

I cock my head to the side. "Is there no one you trust, Sergei?"

"I cannot afford to trust, not when you have more than enough trust for both of us." His tone is bitter, and I feel it like a slap across my face.

"We will ride until we can no longer follow the trail, then stop and make camp for the night. Then we will leave again at first light," I order. "Peter's traveling in a carriage, so we will be able to make up some time. And the Prussian soldiers will come with us. Keep them in front, where we can keep an eye on them, should it come to battle."

Sergei nods curtly and rides away to give the soldiers the news.

By the time we make camp, I can scarcely move.

I'm sore from the saddle, sore from carrying such tension, and sore with worry that we will not find Peter in time. I lay alone in my bed, not willing to risk taking comfort with my lovers with so many eyes fixed on my every move. The wind blows, beating against the damask walls of my tent, an ominous sound that keeps my eyes from fully closing.

When daylight comes, I'm already dressed and ready to ride again. It is only my own will that keeps me moving now, and it will have to sustain me for some time yet, I fear.

We ride on, finally catching up to Peter's entourage at Alexander Palace. The citadel looks largely abandoned, save for Peter's empty carriage and a handful of guards milling about outside. As we approach, they draw swords and rifles, set on defending their king. I ride ahead, offering them the same terms as the last set of troops. One man, a tall commander, snickers and brandishes his sword at me.

In one smooth motion, I draw a knife from my boot and throw it, impaling him square in the chest. He falls to the ground with a surprised mutter. As soon as his body falls, my soldiers ride in, some forming a protective ring around me, others attacking outright. The battle doesn't last long. After the first few bodies fall, the others throw down their swords and rifles. Sergei, after leading the charge, breaks through my protective guard to where I wait, still mounted lest I should need to flee.

"They have thrown up arms and surrendered. Peter is inside."

Exhaling, it's as if the breath is seeping from my very marrow. I never wanted war, never wanted to see men bloodied at my expense. But that is the cost of being empress, and while I know that, seeing it so closely is quite another thing. I ride past the tall, iron gates and into the courtyard before dismounting.

As I make my way up the main stairs and into the wide, gothic parlor, Alexander takes his place beside me, handing me a tightly wound scroll.

"Where is he?" I demand of a white-wigged valet who peeks his head around the corner.

Apparently deciding that dignity is the better part of valor, he steps out, straightening his gold-buttoned jacket. "He's in the West Hall," he says, motioning for us to follow him.

The palace, still unfinished, is a raw shell. The floors are laid, stone walls constructed, but it lacks the detail, the lavish décor and gilded arches, of the other Russian imperial palaces. Tucking the scroll under my arm, I swiftly strip off my riding gloves, handing them off to Sergei, who stands stiff, one hand on his sword as if expecting an ambush. I stop and the valet throws the glass doors open with fervor, stepping aside to let me pass.

Huddled on the floor in a crumpled heap, Peter is absently chewing on the lapel of his coat like a child. His blue eyes are wide, ringed with red, and his face is pale and emaciated. The smell of sour milk and brandy rolls off him in toxic waves, making my eyes water as I approach. They had told him I was coming, surely, and he chose to drink himself into oblivion rather than fight for his country.

For a moment, there is pity that creeps into my heart. I force myself to remember every cruel word, every rough touch, every bruise and cut and every single time I hated him. It buoys me, filling each step with renewed purpose.

This is a hell of his own making.

I tighten my fingers around the scroll until my knuckles are white, the parchment crumpling under the strain. In the corner of the room, Mikhail sits, his head down, his hands folded in his lap. He seems like a man expecting an axe as opposed to forgiveness. Perhaps Sergei is right; perhaps he is dangerous to me. It is a matter I will have to decide later.

Peter looks up at me, his expression that of a dog waiting to be beaten. "I fear I have displeased you, little mother."

Refilled with righteous anger, I say nothing, snapping my fingers to the nearest guard and motioning for a chair to be brought over. He obeys quickly and I fold myself into the seat like a queen, slowly and with a flourish of my riding skirts. Clasping my hands patiently in my lap, I wait in silence.

This seems to unnerve Peter even more. Reaching up, he weaves his fingers into his disheveled blond curls and pulls forcefully, ripping out bloody chunks and offering them to me.

"Is this why you've come? For my blood? It's what you've wanted all along, isn't it?" he spits.

I frown. "If it was simply your blood I wanted, I would have taken that long ago," I answer, no emotion left in my voice. "But you have pushed me, Peter, far beyond what you should have. Now, there is no option left for me—for us—save you giving me what I came for."

He looks away, his eyes fixing on my guards, who wait in the doorway, swords drawn. Licking his lips, he asks, "Have you come to kill me?"

I feel my jaw clench, if only for a moment. Killing him would be the wise thing, the just thing in every respect. Yet somehow, I know that despite all he has done, it isn't in me to kill him. He is deplorable in his patheticness—that much is true. But he is my husband, and I can't shake the feeling that it should count for something at least.

"No, but I think you shall wish I had."

"How is my son?" he asks sadly, his skin waxen in the flickering candlelight. "Do you think he will weep for me when I'm gone?"

A flicker of anger spreads through me like warm water. How dare he even ask such a thing, after all he has done? He never cared for the boy before…

Then I realize his real question. Am I going to allow his son, our son, to live, or am I going to erase their line completely? What a monster he must think I am. Or… perhaps, it is simply what he would have done, had our situations been reversed.

I exhale deeply. "Paul is well. He is the heir, and he is protected."

Peter nods.

Holding up the scroll, I lean forward. Though I'm growing numb to the smell of Peter's stench, night is falling quickly and I hear the horses growing restless outside. There is something in the air that makes me uneasy, a deep, cold resolution of changing skies. The storms are on the horizon, I can feel it in my bones. This must be taken care of before his Holstein reinforcements arrive.

"This is a letter of abdication. You will sign it."

I'm not sure what I expect from him. Once, not so long ago, he would have raged at my demand, but this is not a king, I remind myself. This is a broken boy, a once-beautiful, clever man who has been reduced to the creature before me. He is damaged. Some by my own hand, some by others, some damage from long before I first set eyes on him, but he is beyond repair. Left unchecked, he would burn all of Russia to the ground, and me along with it.

"I never wanted Russia in any case," he says, matter-of-factly. "I belong with my own people; I belong in Prussia. Remember that you never defeated me, wife. I simply refused to fight."

And so, he doesn't rage or fight or scream. He just nods, his expression petulant, and holds out his hand for the scroll.

"If I sign this, you will allow Elizavetta and me to flee to Prussia, unmolested?"

Holding myself perfectly still, I nod once in agreement. Behind me, I feel Sergei bristle, but I ignore it.

He unrolls it and reads aloud. "I, Peter, of my own free will, hereby solemnly declare, not only to the whole of the Russian empire, but also to the world, that I forever renounce the throne of Russia to the end of my days. Nor will I ever seek to recover the same at any time or with anyone's assistance. I swear this before God."

As I watch, he reaches out his other hand, waiting for a quill to be stuffed into it, and then scribbles his name hastily before crawling away, under a nearby table. I look up. Sergei is eyeing him closely as Bestuzhev circles the room, picking up the discarded parchment and adding his initials as a witness. When he holds out the scroll to me, I quickly add my own signature and it's done. The royal seal is applied, and the scroll is laid carefully in a wooden box.

Just like that, in a dark, stagnant sitting room in Alexander Palace, I have taken the last of it. Everything he had or was or might have been, now belongs to me. His name, his crown, his country, his wealth, it is all mine.

I know it's a great victory, but even as everyone in the room, friend and foe, begins to drop to one knee with a cry of "Long Live the Queen," it doesn't feel like a victory at all, and I can't stop staring at Peter's beady blue eyes glowering at me from under that table.

It's Sergei who helps me to my feet. Releasing his hand quickly, I avoid his gaze. I know he thinks I should strike Peter down this moment, he's said as much time and again. As a matter of fact, it seems to be one of the few things he and Alexander agree on. Their argument is sound. After all, Elizabeth let young Ivan live and it haunted her until the day she died. There is so little of my humanity left, I cannot bear to waste it on Peter. Sergei levels his gaze at me; his expression is one of steely warning. It's a warning I've chosen not to heed.

I sweep through the palace in a flourish. Near the top of the stairs, I see the guards are holding a woman by the arms. Though she isn't facing me, her long, orange-red hair gives her away. My anger bubbles once more inside me. Peter, perhaps, is too sad to bring me to such hatred, but she, she who is the cause of so many of my pains, is quite another matter. Before I can think of what I'm doing, I'm climbing the steps, slowly, ferocity growing with each foothold.

"Elizavetta," I call. "Stand aside."

She turns and immediately, my heart sinks into my bowels. She is plump and pink faced as usual, but her belly is round with child. It seems I was not the only one hiding a pregnancy these past months. She strokes her stomach and glares at me.

"What you have done here is of no consequence. Peter will be king once again, and he will make me his queen. Our child will sit on the throne of Russia," she spits, her voice thick with venom.

I wave the guards away. "Give us a moment."

Sergei puts a hand on my shoulder, but I brush it away. I watch him canter down the stairs, Alexander offering me a sidelong glance as he follows. The rest of my entourage is not far behind them. Once they are gone, I circle her like a hawk about to dive for prey.

"Peter has abdicated. You, nor your child, will ever sit on the throne," I say, trying to fight back the rage slowly building inside me. "You will waste away in whatever prison I decide to throw Peter into, and your child will never be allowed to see the light of day. Is that the shining future you hoped for when you stole Peter from me? Was it worth all the years you spent bending over for a man so addled that he couldn't even be bothered to officially claim his own throne?"

She smirks, taking a step forward. "You will fail. Peter will gather troops from Prussia, and they will send what's left of you and your child back to Germany in a box."

My resolve cracks and I strike out, grabbing her by the wrist. "You took my husband. You killed my first child because you saw how it was bringing us together. You told Elizabeth about my plan to run away with Alexander before the wedding."

"Of course I did! Though I see now I should have let you run off to Denmark and ruin yourself for that wretched nobody. Then I would have been queen from the start."

We are shouting now, and though she tries to wrench herself free, I hold her fast.

"You stole my life. My every chance at happiness. You killed my child." My voice is no longer my own. Fury rises inside me like a tide I cannot struggle against.

"And I would do it again!" she screams.

The smugness melts from her face, replaced by a look of shock—and fear—as she realizes what she's said. Her cheeks pale, her mouth snapping shut like a bear trap. I tighten my hand around her wrist until she cries out in pain. Burning behind her eyes is a determination I've never noticed before. Peter is dangerous only as a figurehead, as a political puppet. She is dangerous in the way only a woman can be. She will see me and my children dead if the chance arises; there's no doubt in my mind.

I'm not sure what comes over me in that moment. Years of buried hate, resentment, and rage froth to the surface, clouding everything else. In that moment, there is true darkness in my soul and all I want, more than anything in the world, is to watch the life bleed from her eyes.

And I jerk her arm.

At first, I'm not sure what's happened; the move is so much an unthinking reflex. But as I watch her begin to fall, I know I could stop her. I could reach out, take her now-outstretched hand, and save them both.

But I don't.

Watching her fall slows time down inside my mind. I remember my own fall down such a similar staircase. Time slows around me, the present slipping away into my memories. I remember crushing blows one after another as my body rolled down step by step. I remember the feel of her hands on my back, the pain ripping through me as I prayed for death, and most of all, I remember waking to discover my child had been lost. Sergei's child.

By the time the world snaps back into focus, it's far too late. She tumbles, a blur of red hair and blue silk, down the stairs, finally hitting the bottom with a thick crunch. I don't take my eyes off her as I descend the stairs, getting closer and closer to her crumpled body. By the time I reach the bottom, a small pool of blood has formed under her head, and her lifeless eyes are wide. Numb to what has just happened, I step over her, lifting my skirts to avoid the blood.

I know I should feel something. Guilt, remorse, even satisfaction. But there's nothing. Just a deadness tingling through my entire body as I walk past her, not looking back. When I open the doors, Sergei looks past me at the horrifying scene and takes me by the arm.

"Are you all right?" he asks, not taking his eyes off her still body.

"It was she who killed our child," I whisper. "It was she who pushed me down the stairs so long ago. I always believed it was, but to hear her speak the words…" Glancing back over my shoulder, I frown. "I don't think I meant to do it. Or maybe I did. I can't be sure."

From somewhere, a dry laugh rises, slipping free from my lips before I can stop it. It's only then that he looks at me, fully and in the face, his eyes swirling with concern. I pull myself free of him.

Turning to Grigori, I raise my hand. "Seize Peter. Tie him and throw him on a horse. He will be taken to the citadel for imprisonment, indefinitely." He obeys without hesitation. Behind me, Peter mewls like a whimpering child. The sound is grating. I find I can stand it no longer, so I run from the hall and out into the grey dusk.

"You promised him freedom," Alexander whispers as he comes to my side.

I rake my hands through my hair. "I know. I made a promise I couldn't possibly keep. You know what that's like, don't you?"

He jerks back, surprised by my harsh words. I shake my head. "No, I'm sorry. I didn't mean that. I just feel so adrift."

He takes my hand gently, grazing a kiss across my knuckles. "Then let me be your anchor, at least during this storm."

No sooner do I nod than the sky lets loose, rain falling cold against my skin. I only have a few moments to let it wash over me before Alexander hoists me onto my horse, shoving the reins in my cold hands. I don't wait for the others. Kicking my mare into a full gallop, I ride as if I can outrun the devil himself.

We ride hard and fast through the beating rain back to the Winter Palace. I'm so cold and wet that I'm shaking all over but I never stop, never slow my pace. The rain rolls down my face like holy baptism until I can't even tell if I'm crying.

Chapter
SEVENTEEN

I waste no time riding into the fortress of Peter and Paul. There is no one waiting for me in the driving rain save for a handful of guards, who usher me inside. At my left, Alexander steps forward, presenting the Archbishop of Novgorod with the wooden box containing the scroll. I fall to my knees before him, part humility, part exhaustion. He reads the mandate aloud to the gathered Synod and council members before taking me by the hand and leading me to the golden iconostas that arches above us and into the bell tower. As he begins his chanting, the storm breaks. The afternoon light filters through the tall, stained glass windows, illuminating the cathedral in shards of red, blue, and green. The gathered crowd is so quiet that his words echo through the room as he pronounces me Gosudarina, the sovereign ruler of Russia.

Each attendee takes a moment to offer me a blessing as well as their fervent oath of loyalty. Perhaps it is having seen them offer the same loyalty to Peter, only to then watch as they each, in turn, turned on him, that makes their pledges feel empty. I know that their loyalty, their support, will come only so long as I continue to earn it, to prove each day that I am worthy of their devotion. Perhaps that is the biggest difference between Peter and me. He thought himself owed their love. I know I will have to earn it over and over.

By the time the rest of my group arrives, I am already mounting for the trek back to Winter Palace. I will not stop in the square, but rather address the crowd from the great balcony of the palace, my son in my arms.

Alexander rides ahead, to set the final preparations into motion. By the time I arrive, Dash has dry clothes set out and little Paul is waiting in my chamber, playing with a wooden train with his nurse. I kiss him gently atop the head and retire to change.

My legs quake beneath me, threatening to give out at any moment. By the time I arrive at the balcony, Lord Grey, along with Prince George and Mikhail himself, are addressing the crowd. They attest that I, Catherine II, being moved by the perils facing Russia from a shameful dependence of foreign powers, and sustained by divine providence, have yielded to the outcries of my people that I should ascend the throne. When I step forward, Paul on my hip, the crowd greets me with riotous cheers. I raise a hand to calm them, but it is of no use. The crowd is thick from palace square, as far as the eye can see.

With my chin up, I simply say, "My faithful subjects, you have prayed earnestly for liberation from the dark days that have followed us since the death of Empress Elizabeth. It is my humble offer that I will lead you once more into the light. And I present to you, my son, and the rightful heir of the Imperial throne, Paul Petrovitch of Russia."

Cheers double, creating a thunderous sound. Church bells ring out, and Paul covers his ears against the noise. Ducking back inside, I release him to his nurse and turn to Grigori.

"I must do one more thing this day. I must visit the soldiers. Gather the house guard, the infantry, and any nearby regiments. I will meet them at Peterhof, at the head of the Horse guard," I say, the first hints of exhaustion seeping into my voice.

Dash and I change once more, into Preobrazhensky uniforms, the uniforms of the old guard, before Peter ordered them into their silly Prussian-inspired attire. Mine fits well, but Dash's makes her look like a young boy, something that seems to make her giddy with delight. Leaving my poor, hard-ridden mare Peony to rest, I mount the largest white stallion and lead my men on the road toward Peterhoff. People gather in the streets to watch us pass, some running up to kiss my boot or the hem of my jacket.

It's slow going, but we make it to the grounds at Peterhoff before nightfall, and at my count, nearly fourteen thousand men await my arrival. A handful of men approach me, their faces flushed.

"Beg forgiveness, Your Majesty. We would have joined you at the Winter Palace, but some of our generals would not allow it. We have arrested them, you see." They motion proudly to where four men stand tied in a tight ring.

Reaching down, I touch the head of the one speaking. "Your loyalty is appreciated."

They all cheer as I dismount, Grigori close by my side. "Have those four generals brought to my tent. I would speak with them," I say flatly.

"Of course. But first," he pauses, waving his hand toward the assembled masses, "your army awaits your inspection."

Taking a deep breath, I nod and head for the first regiment.

I sleep only a few hours on a small cot, Dash curled beside me in the tent outside of Peterhoff. But the men are eager to return to St. Petersburg, so we ride out before dawn. As before, the streets are crowded with people. Only now, I ride into the city with thousands of soldiers at my back, a sight startling enough to make anyone quiver with awe. When I return to my chamber, the maids are already moving my things into the Imperial apartments—

the rooms that once belonged to Elizabeth. I'm too tired to stop them, so I simply allow myself to fall into bed.

It is nearly a full day later when I wake to find the transition well in hand. George has sent letters to every foreign ruler alerting them to the coup, as well as sending agents to the wharf to alert all ships and dock workers to the new sovereign. I find he is quite good at these things and consider keeping him on as part of my new Privy council. Days pass in upheaval, the old house guard replaced, Peter's Prussian soldiers sent back to Holstein—save for the few who volunteered to remain as members of the new Russian army—and new ladies-in-waiting are assigned. Soon, we have formal alliances with every nation from France to Denmark, and old wounds are finally beginning to heal.

"Where is Peter now?" I ask, shuffling the papers around my massive oak desk.

"He was complaining of the conditions, so he's been taken to Ropsha, a secluded house in the country. There's a lake, as well as pastures for him to walk around," Alexander answers through gritted teeth. "Though I don't know why you go to such trouble to see that he is comfortable. Surely, he never gave you such consideration."

I pause, looking up from my work. "He has been in custody for months and he has sent me letters nearly every day, each begging me to reunite him with Elizavetta. He still believes I will eventually release them both to Prussia," I answer, my heart leaden. "Not only have I lied to him, but I have stolen from him the thing he holds most dear in life. Do you not imagine that is suffering enough for his sins?"

Alexander's answer is firm and unwavering. "No."

"We could send him to Schlusselburg for confinement," Sergei offers.

I shake my head. "No, it's too close to the city. Besides, that is where Ivan was kept, and I saw first-hand what that sort of confinement can do to a person's mind."

"Either way, you cannot deny the need to rid yourself of him. Even dethroned and imprisoned he remains, in the eyes of God, your lawful husband," Alexander adds, his voice monotone.

That gives me pause, and I set my quill in the inkwell. "And you imagine I should murder my husband so that I might be free to take another?" I glance between them. "I suppose I know which of my lovers you believe should take his place." His face falls, and I know I've been too harsh. "I will not stoop to the depth that Peter would have in my place. He will live out his days, as comfortably as I can allow, far from court. And that is my final word on the matter."

Neither man seems pleased with my decree, but the matter is dropped.

Chapter

EIGHTEEN

Though I'm far too busy with matters of state—mostly consisting of cleaning up Peter's messes—to handle the details myself, Chancellor Bestuzhev spares no expense in preparing for my coronation. There was some concern about returning him to the post he'd served for so long, but with all the other changes, I liked the idea of returning some of the old guard, as it were, and when he took his vow of loyalty to me, there was no doubt of his sincerity. I offered the post first to Mikhail, but he refused. I think he simply spent so much of his life dancing to Peter's ever-fluid tune, that he dreamt of leaving court far behind. I gave him a small parcel of land near Peterhoff and kopecks enough to live out his days quite comfortably.

I allow myself to be pulled from my office for the first time in days as Jean and his assistants begin preparing me for the ceremony. My hair is still quite short, but many of the noble ladies of court cut their hair to match the fashion. Even Dash trimmed off nearly a foot of her long, golden locks to remain in style.

The gown is dreadfully heavy, much worse than my wedding gown. It's gold and silver threads and embroidered with the twin-headed crowned eagle, the symbol of the Romanov house. A reminder for all that, unlike Peter before me, I stand for Russia. When they drape it over my wide-caged panniers, I think I might collapse from the strain.

"I hear women in France are adding tiny, wheeled carts in their undergarments to help support the weight," Dash offers jovially.

The side of my lips turns up, imagining the French queen rolling herself down the hall on such a contraption. "I'm sure it works quite well, until one is faced with the issue of stairs."

We both laugh and it feels refreshing, as if it's for the first time in years.

A specially crafted cape of red and white fur trails behind me as I make my way down the aisle of Kazan Cathedral, the same place where I had been converted and ordained Catherine II. The priests sing and chant, and the room is filled with burnt frankincense wafting in white clouds. Every inch of me is draped in gold and jewels. My legs quake under the strain as I slowly march forward. The whole day has been a blur of activity, only now, in the relative silence, do I have a moment to pause and take a breath. As I kneel at the altar, they anoint me and bless me, finally hefting the diamond-and ruby-laden crown onto my head to thunderous applause.

I'm too preoccupied to truly enjoy the ceremony. Odd, since I'd worked so hard to arrive at this precise moment, but it all falls away as I search for a familiar face in the audience, only to be disappointed. A fleeting moment of panic clutches me and I have visions of Holstein troops bursting down the doors of the church, Peter striding in on horseback, declaring my claim to the throne invalid. It doesn't happen, of course, but I don't feel the tension leave my shoulders until I'm safely back in my carriage. I exhale, handing my cape to Dashka.

"Where are Sergei and Alexander?" I ask, watching out the window as the guard surrounds the carriage and the royal procession begins its journey back to the palace. "I didn't see them at the ceremony. They didn't come to breakfast either."

She doesn't answer right away, instantly drawing my suspicion. I glance at her, and she is fiddling with the cloth in her lap.

"Where is Sergei?" I demand.

She takes a deep breath and releases it before answering. "I can't say, Your Majesty."

I lick my lips. "And where is Alexander?"

She shakes her head again.

I snap my fingers. "You must tell me, now."

Visions of their capture dance in my head. My dear Sergei bound and beaten, blood covering his rugged face. Alexander, his dark eyes staring up at me vacantly from the ground. Though the chancellor assures me that Peter's forces have all but crumbled, there is always an uncertainty in his voice that frightens me. If they have been taken...

No, I can't even entertain the thought.

"I believe they left the palace only last night, Your Majesty. I do not know where they went."

"And they left, together?" I ask.

She nods, but she doesn't meet my gaze.

I swallow my doubts as we reach the main road where the people have lined up to watch the procession pass. Leaning forward to be visible through the window of the carriage, I smile and wave to my people as we pass even as my stomach churns with worry.

Chapter
NINETEEN

SERGEI

Night has only just fallen when I reach the stable. Alexander and I are preparing to ride out under the cover of darkness. He's already there, saddling the horses.

"She'll never forgive us for this, you know?" he asks, not looking at me.

I laugh dryly. "For which, killing Peter or missing her coronation?"

"Both," he answers with a forced smile.

"She is young and far too softhearted for her own good. And so it falls to lesser men to keep her safe—whatever the cost," I finally say, stepping into the stirrups and throwing my leg across the saddle.

"Then we will have to hope she is softhearted enough not to have us flogged," he mutters as we ride off.

The night stretches on before us. Only my own knowledge of these roads keeps us from going astray, that and the soft glow from the full moon overhead. When we finally reach Ropsha, the sun is once more climbing high in the sky. I'm sore from the ride, but determined to press onward. As quietly as possible, we dismount in the woods on the northern edge of the property and slink through the trees.

To call it a modest country home would be a mistake. Ropsha estate sprawls for nearly thirty acres, lavish green gardens to the east, an apple orchard to the west, and between us and the front entrance, a massive marble fountain spews water twenty feet in the air. Beyond that is a stone staircase leading to the doors. Outside, two guards stand watch. I narrow my eyes, looking closely. They are speaking to each other, their shoulders hunched, their rifles propped against the building. They don't expect attack. Why should they? Catherine has ordered Peter to be kept like a prince rather than a prisoner of war.

Closing my eyes only for a moment, I let thoughts of her fill my mind. I think of the way she chews her bottom lip when she's reading, about the sound she makes right before she falls asleep, about the vicious tongue lashing I'll receive upon my return. I can't help but smile at the images as they float through my head. How one woman can possess so many facets, I will never understand. I knew from the moment I laid eyes on her that she would capture me, body and soul, and she did. The first night she came to me—her wedding night—so determined to best Peter and Elizabeth, so full of fire and passion. She had me from that moment, if not before.

When I open my eyes again, one of the guards is leaving. A changing of duty, perhaps. *Good.* One guard will be easier to deal with than two at any rate. Beside me, Alexander anxiously shifts. He doesn't have the stomach for violence—that much is clear. I've often wondered if it is that high morality that drew Catherine to him, like a moth to flame. Perhaps she sees in him a quality that she lacks but seeks to emulate.

Personally, I find him short-tempered and soft. Unable to do what must be done. Yet here he is, ready to do the unthinkable, just to keep her safe.

Perhaps I have not given him enough credit.

"Do we wait for nightfall?" he asks, glancing around the forest floor.

I shake my head. "No. It must be done today. Catherine will be standing blameless before the whole of Russia when Peter dies, perfectly unaware and innocent of this deed."

"Then we ride in, feigning a message from court?"

I lick my bottom lip. Truthfully, I'd rather not be seen at all. Catherine would want as little bloodshed as possible, and so we cannot risk being seen, having our involvement reported. "No, we will go in through the kitchens. Anyone who sees our faces..."

I don't say more and though he visibly pales at

the implication, he nods firmly.

We circle the house, leaving the horses tied in the woods at the rear of the estate, and make our way up through the gardens. Letting the tall juniper maze provide our cover, we slip into the kitchens unseen.

In the rear of the house, we come upon the guard's chamber and steal inside. The guard who recently left his post is inside, changing his shirt, when Alexander comes up behind him, wraps his arm around the man's thick neck, and chokes him. The guard struggles only a few moments, unable to draw breath to call for assistance before falling unconscious to the floor.

Without speaking, we slip into a spare set of uniform jackets and hats and creep back into the hallway, careful to keep our chins down.

"Split up," I order. "You take the east wing, I'll take the west. We'll—" I don't get to finish my words because the door in front of us opens and a maid steps out, cursing loudly.

"Perhaps next time you'll eat something more than a bottle of whiskey then!" she shouts, slamming the door behind her.

From behind the door, Peter's voice carries. "How dare you speak to me in such a way! I am the king!"

As she brushes past, the maid mutters, "The king of chaffing my arse."

I have to force down a snicker at her exasperation. Once the maid rounds the corner, I glance up
at Alexander. Sweat has beaded up along his forehead and nose, his face pale but his expression determined.

He nods once and I push the door open, drawing my sword with one hand as I shut the door with
the other, latching the lock.

Peter turns. For a moment, he looks confused,
and then he sighs, throwing himself across the wide,
silk-covered bed to grab a small, wooden sword hidden beneath the blankets.

"Finally. I knew my wife would come to her senses. I'll call for the valet to begin packing my things,"
he says, standing slowly.

Alexander looks to me, and then back to Peter,
who freezes mid-step.

"Where is Elizavetta? Have you brought her to
me? Even Catherine would not be so cruel as to
keep us apart. Surely, she doesn't hate me so much,"
he begs.

I step forward to run him through before he can
realize our true purpose and scream for help, but
Alexander speaks too quickly. "Elizavetta is dead,"
he says flatly.

In the blink of an eye, I lunge, but Peter uses his
wooden sword to block my own, his eyes widening
with feral rage. Dropping his shoulder, he lunges at
me, knocking me off balance. I fall into the wall.

He lands another blow before Alexander grabs him from behind, shoving his sword into Peter's back and through his chest. A trickle of blood falls from his open mouth as Peter looks down, examining the blade, which is slippery with his own blood.

Releasing him, Alexander takes a step back, leaving the sword behind. Peter must realize what's just happened because he looks up at me and smiles, then rushes forward.

I hear Alexander scream a moment too late. The blade pierces flesh, cutting through my ribs as Peter wraps his arms around me, holding me in a deadly embrace.

The last things I hear as we fall to the floor are Peter's gasping words in my ear.

"She has taken my heart from me. Now I return the favor."

Chapter

TWENTY

CATHERINE

I've still not recovered from what I've done to Elizavetta. Her face haunts my dreams, and I wake crying out, as if to stop myself. But I cannot. It is a weight I must carry, like so many others, on my tarnished soul. Nearly throwing myself from my bed, I fight to shake off the nightmare. Dawn is risen, and the smell of fresh coffee slips through the air. I dress myself quickly, taking an extra moment to affix my crown into my hair.

Throwing the doors wide, I see Alexander is standing by the fireplace, his expression distant.

I move to embrace him. "You missed the coronation. What could be so important…?"

I don't get to finish my thought. He turns, and the front of his suit is covered in blood. It's my nightmare happening right before my eyes.

My head snaps up and I open my mouth to speak, but he holds up his hands. "It's not my blood.

I'm all right."

"Thank heavens," I say, rushing to him and throwing myself in his arms despite myself. "I was afraid some of Peter's supporters had—"

He cuts me off with a kiss. It's slow and sad and when I pull away, I see fear in his eyes.

"What is it?" I demand. "What's happened?"

He gently strokes the side of my cheek, staring hard at me, as if trying to memorize my face. "Peter is dead."

I feel myself step back in shock. "Dead? How?"

His dark eyes flutter closed, and I feel my heart stutter in my chest. "You?" I whisper.

He nods. I step back again, turning away from him as my fury rises. My hands move to my hair, meaning to tug on it, but end up on my crown instead. I lift it gently and set it on my table. The feel of it in my hands helps me focus.

"I told you that I wanted him left alive. This, this is… How could you defy me like this?"

"He was a danger to you. We couldn't allow him to—"

Now it is my turn to cut him off. "We? Who went with you?" Then it dawns on me. "Sergei." I whisper his name like a curse. Of course. The only thing that could possibly unite them would be their desire to protect me. "Where is he?" I demand, ready to share my rage between them.

He doesn't answer. Instead, he holds out his

hands to me. I watch as grief plays out across his features, and then my eyes fall back to the blood on his tunic. Looking down at myself, I see that the stain spread to me when I embraced him. I touch the crimson flakes gently with my fingertips, unable to quite believe what my mind is trying to tell me. Dry blood falls to the floor like crimson snow.

Realization hits me quickly, taking my already shaky legs from under me. I fall to the floor, my gown cascading around me in heaps of fabric. The air rushes from my lungs, and I can't seem to force myself to take a replenishing breath. I can't even gasp, the crushing tightness wrapping around my chest. In a fit, I rip at my clothes. I can't breathe; I have to get out of my corset or I will surely die. My mind reels, white stars exploding behind my eyes. The sound of tearing fabric and the frantic pounding of my own heart is all I can hear.

I think I'm screaming.

My throat is raw and while I can't hear the sound, my throat fights to create it.

Seeing my distress, Alexander falls to his knees and begins ripping away the fabric with his strong hands. Finally, when it's hanging in shreds around my waist, he produces a short sword from his belt and cuts me free of the laces, discarding the corset with a careless toss. I slap at his hands, not wanting him to touch me, not wanting to look into his face. I want to scratch, claw, and fight my way free of this nightmare. But it's too late. I fall forward, gasping for short, labored breaths, as the room around me fades to white.

Is this what it feels like to die? I wonder.

Then I feel his lips, forcing air from his lungs into mine. Part of me wants to wrap my arms around his neck, to let him hold me as I once had, but another, darker part pushes him away, ill at the thought of his kiss. There's something between us now, a wall that will never be broken or torn down. I can feel it rising, brick by brick around my heart.

With one feeble hand, I push him away and manage to draw in a breath on my own. I hear him cry out for help and the heavy boot steps of my guard rush in. I feel a warm hand taking mine, and the sensation of being lifted into the air and carried to my bed.

As I blink rapidly, the fog begins to fade. Grigori, my guard, is beside my bed, sword drawn, standing between Alexander and me.

"I'm sorry, I'm sorry. Please forgive me," Alexander mutters over and over, tears falling down his beautiful face.

How I love him. How much I wish I didn't.

When I speak, my voice is hoarse, but unwavering. "Tell me what happened; tell me all of it this instant."

He raises his hands in surrender, his eyes falling to the floor. "We knew you would never truly be safe so long as Peter lived. So Sergei and I made a plan to go to the estate during your coronation and put an end to him."

"He was your friend once," I whisper.

His eyes dart up, searching my own. "He was a monster. He would have slaughtered you without hesitation. As long as he drew breath, you were in danger. We only wanted you to be safe, finally, and free."

I say nothing as he continues.

"When we got there, we snuck into his chamber. He was demanding to know where Elizavetta was and…" He hesitates, his words failing. "He flew into a rage. He attacked Sergei. I stabbed him, but with his last breath he… he killed Sergei. He ran him through. I'm so sorry. So sorry."

Even as the last unbroken pieces of my heart shatter, my mind reels. Pain and anger builds inside me, crashing against my chest in bitter waves.

"Convenient for you, isn't it? For my husband and my lover, the only men you ever had to share me with, both gone in a single instant." I pause, letting the anger freely course through me. "I wonder—did you even try to save Sergei? Or did you finally see an opportunity to have me all to yourself?"

He sputters. "Of course I tried to save him. How could you even think such a thing?"

I stare at him, a cold fury sliding across my skin. "Was it a blade that killed Sergei? I gave strict orders he wasn't to have access to knives or swords of any kind. So where did he get the blade, and do not think to lie to me."

He freezes at my words, finally answering in a defeated tone. "It was my blade, the blade I stabbed Peter with. He used it to kill Sergei. But it was not my intent, whatever you think."

"You have betrayed me. I gave you an order, and you *betrayed* me. Your betrayal cost me the life of someone I loved as well as if you'd murdered him with your own hand!" Conflicting emotions rage inside me. He betrayed me, defied me. He put Peter's blood on my hands, and Sergei's too. The panic rises once more as I realize I will never see his face again. I will never stare into his warm, blue-green eyes, will never again find safety in his arms. Inside the newly formed wall, the battered pieces of my heart ache. I want to forgive Alexander, but I can't. I can't trust that he didn't let Sergei die just to see me free of him. He killed Peter to keep me safe, would he kill Sergei to keep me for himself? I do not know, and that is the worst part. I want to trust him, but I cannot. The wound is too deep.

"You broke my heart," I say, my voice barely a whisper.

He moves to challenge Grigori, as if he wants nothing more than to fight his way to my side. But the damage is done. I sit up, steeling myself.

"Lord Alexander Mananov, I am ordering you

from Imperial Court. You will return to Denmark, effective immediately. Is that clear?"

The shock on his face is plain. "You're sending me away?" he asks, his voice broken.

"I cannot trust you at my side any longer. Your feelings for me have overcome your better judgment. I am not a girl who needs saving, I am a queen—your queen—and you will do as you are told." My tone is cold, unforgiving. It must be, or he will never go. It's more than not trusting him to do what I say; it's trusting myself not to be ruled by him. I would lose myself in him if I could. I know that well enough. He has been a font from which I took my strength. But that font is tainted, and I will have to learn to find strength inside myself now.

He says nothing, just stares at me, first in disbelief, and then in resignation. It's all I have not to call him back. Finally, he bows and turns away. As soon as he does, I close my eyes, struggling to hold a perfect image of him in my mind. A time when he was smiling, his dark eyes dancing with joy, and I was lying in his arms. I cling to it like a drowning man might cling to a raft.

When he leaves, with Grigori close at his heels, I turn over in my bed, stripping off the last bits of my gown. The tingling numbness floods my body, making its way through my skin, deep into my very bones, which feel as hollow as the rest of me. Shaking and in silence, I watch the sun begin to set through my window until my maids come to prepare me for the evening's feast.

Dashka is first in the room. She curls into the bed with me, wrapping her arms around me and holding me until the shaking stops. Finally, she brushes my hair back and tucks it over my ear.

"It's time, Your Majesty," she says softly. "We will go and reassure everyone that all is as it should be. You will be strong and radiant, and then later, if you need to, we will cry ourselves to sleep."

Drawing myself from my bed, I stand, squaring my shoulders, my chin high as I push the last of the grief aside, burying it deep beneath a layer of other things. My own pain is no longer relevant. All that matters now is Russia. It is all that I have left.

"No, Dash. No more tears. No more grief. I am a queen now, the Empress of Russia. And I must set those childish emotions aside. It is time to do what I was born to do. It is time to rule."

I go about the motions, bathing and dressing, letting them curl and powder my hair, paint my face, and cover me in jewels and ribbons, all while discussing my schedule with my valet and dictating letters to be sent to my foreign allies. Inside, it's as if I've been emptied out. All traces of the girl I was are gone, and all that remains is this. Finally, I hold my gaze in the mirror, looking for any traces of young Sophie of Prussia, but they are long gone now. Only the empress remains, staring back at me with cold,

dark eyes. When they lift the crown onto my head
once more, I say a silent prayer for the girl I'd been,
for the woman I am, and for the queen I have become.

GOD SAVE THE QUEEN.

Epilogue

To my dearest children,

If you are reading this letter, then I have passed through this life into the waiting arms of my Lord God. I write you now, having never enjoyed the opportunity in life to express myself fully to you, because I know all too well the things that have been said about me, the rumors, innuendo, and the wild speculation, and I wish you to know the plain truth of my life.

Life, for me, has been fraught with hardship and also blessed with great joy. To know one is to, inevitably, feel the other. I have no regrets, save one. I know I was not the mother you deserved. The weight of the crown and the demands of my station prevented me from taking the role I would have liked to in your lives. For that, I am deeply sorry. But you were loved nonetheless, and with every fiber of my being.

My husband Peter was a man who was never fit to be king. His mind was addled and his soul darkened long before I met him, and that darkness only grew as the wariness of the world descended upon him. I never wished him ill, though. I would have stood by his side till the end of my days, if only he would have allowed it. Perhaps I never forgave him for not being the man I dreamed of, the man I needed him to be, when I came to Russia as a young, naive girl. I know certainly that he never forgave me for being the stronger, smarter, more courageous of us. Perhaps that might have made some difference between us, if we had only been able to forgive each other. But it was not to be. I want you to know I had no hand in his death. It was not by my order, and those involved were severely punished. In that matter, at least, my hands are clean.

I know that you, Paul, have the most resentment in your heart toward me. You were such a sweet babe, stolen from my arms by the empress, who could never have children of her own. I hated her for taking you from me, but as you grew, I could see so much of your father in your eyes that it pained me to look at you. I am so sorry for the rift I created between us. Can you ever forgive me? I hope you can let go of past hurts and move forward with a pure heart. Russia belongs to you now, and I hope you will be good to her, and that she will be good to you in return.

Alexei, I have been less of a mother to you than you deserved. My only joy came from knowing you were safe and well loved, far from the damage and lies of court. You were, in a world of deceit and darkness, my one perfect light, untainted by the bleakness of a royal life. Though I sent him away, I loved your father *until the day he died, and I go to my grave loving him still. You are a product of that love and I hope you know how very special that makes you.*

Elizabeth, your father was a man very dear to me, a man I respected, a man I came to love long after I was sure there was no love left in the world for me. Be proud to bear the Orloff name. Grigori was as much a king as any man ever has been.

Know, my sweet children, that I go to meet my maker having loved, and been loved, to the depths of my soul. I have also suffered so much, fought so hard, to secure your futures. I have sacrificed things you will never know and surrendered things you will never understand. Know that I have always, and in all things, tried to do my best. My choices were not always easy, they were not always pleasant, but they were always mine, and mine alone.

Be firm in your faith and steadfast in your morality, know that you are of the divine tree and are born to be kings and queens. Be kind and generous when you are able, but don't be afraid to stand firm when necessary. Read, drink, love, learn, bask in the glory of life, and remember always that I am with you.

All my love,
Catherine

Acknowledgements

There are a great many people who helped me along this process, and I need to take a minute to thank them.

Firstly, Marya, Courtney, and Rebecca from CTP, you gals are amazing. Thanks for taking a chance on my strange little idea and for the stunning covers, marketing, formatting, and general hand-holding you did the whole way. You are amazing!

For my editor, Cynthia Shepp and her team, you guys are the best. If people could see what my first drafts look like, they would fall at your feet because you make my words shine and it wouldn't be half the book it is without you.

For the wonderful bloggers who continue to support me, you are so amazing and I am a very lucky girl to have such amazing friends in my life.

For my writers group, thanks for always being there to listen to my crazy ideas and first-world problems. Thanks for all the caffeine, love, and support. Thank you.

As always, thanks to my family, who prop me up and make me reach for the stars. Especially thanks to my husband, who knows when to bring home tacos and when to just get out of the house for a few days. I LOVE YOU, babe!

And finally, thank you to all the readers who picked up these books and took this journey with me. This isn't just Catherine's story anymore, it's our story now too, and I hope that a little bit of Catherine's courageous spirit lives on inside of each of us.

Chin up. Crown On. Move forward.

XOXP,
~Sherry

About the Author

Sherry D. Ficklin is a full time writer from Colorado where she lives with her husband, four kids, two dogs, and a fluctuating number of chickens and house guests. A former military brat, she loves to travel and meet new people. She can often be found browsing her local bookstore with a large white hot chocolate in one hand and a towering stack of books in the other. That is, unless she's on deadline at which time she, like the Loch Ness monster, is only seen in blurry photographs.

WWW.SHERRYFICKLIN.COM